The camp was overrun

"Where's my blasted HE!" Reese yelled.

"This is Red Leg Five Niner—the HE's coming up. Out."

The first of the 155 mm howitzer illumination rounds burst over the patrol base with a faint pop. The flickering yellow-white flare descending on its parachute illuminated a scene straight out of hell.

Dark figures, their AKs blazing green tracers, scrambled over the ladders and mats thrown on top of the rolls of concertina wire. Claymores exploded with bright flashes, and the dark figures screamed when the steel balls ripped through their ranks, but more of their comrades took their place.

As soon as the first artillery flare flickered and died, two more popped into life above the camp and the hellish scene came to life again. Now the artillery HE rounds were falling, but they were falling at the base of the hill...too far away to do any good.

HATCHET
BLACK MISSION

Knox Gordon

A GOLD EAGLE BOOK FROM
WORLDWIDE®

TORONTO • NEW YORK • LONDON
AMSTERDAM • PARIS • SYDNEY • HAMBURG
STOCKHOLM • ATHENS • TOKYO • MILAN
MADRID • WARSAW • BUDAPEST • AUCKLAND

For Patrick: Gentleman, Scholar, Tanker, Comrade in Arms.

First edition February 1992

ISBN 0-373-63204-5

Special thanks and acknowledgment to
Michael Kasner for his contribution to this work.

BLACK MISSION

BLACK MISSION

Author's Note

Peace talks have nothing to do with peace. Instead, they have to do with war, usually with the termination of a war. They can, however, also be used with deadly effectiveness as a weapon of war. The United States and the Empire of Japan were engaged in "Peace Talks" when the Vals, Kates and Zeros of the Imperial Japanese Navy's First Air Fleet struck the American ships anchored in Pearl Harbor on the morning of Sunday, 7 December 1941.

But it was the North Vietnamese who perfected the art of employing peace talks as a powerful weapon during the Vietnam War.

These talks were first initiated in Paris in May 1968 after the Communists' Tet Offensive failed to conquer South Vietnam. For weeks, the North Vietnamese negotiators argued about the shape of the table they would sit at. While this political bickering was going on, the war in Vietnam continued. Particularly the war along the Vietnamese border where the NVA could hit and then run back to the safety of their sanctuaries in the supposedly neutral nations of Laos and Cambodia.

Once the shape of the table had finally been agreed upon, the peace talks began, but it was obvious from the start that the North Vietnamese were using the talks as a media propaganda theater rather than as a serious attempt to find a way to end the fighting. When they were losing on the battlefield, they talked. When they were winning, though, they walked out.

The peace talks continued until December 1972, when Nixon's Christmas bombing campaign, Linebacker II, succeeded in pounding the North Vietnamese into submission and the peace treaty was finally signed on 27 January 1973.

In the end, the peace treaty proved to be worth less than the paper it was printed on. As soon as the North Vietnamese had built up the required military strength, they violated the treaty by invading South Vietnam in 1975. The American government also violated the terms of the treaty when they failed to support the South Vietnamese government in the face of this massive invasion as they had promised to do.

In the long, hard-fought struggle for freedom in South East Asia, the peace talks proved to be the winning weapon for the Communists.

1

June 28, 1968, Dak Sang, RVN

About two and a half miles east of the South Vietnamese-Cambodian border a small hill squatted in the middle of a narrow valley running from the high mountains along the border, east down into the plains around Pleiku.

Since the dawn of time the valley had been home to wild game. Early men had followed the animals into the valley and remembered it as a good place to hunt. Over the centuries they returned again and again to camp on the hilltop. No one knew what the original inhabitants of this region had called the hill, or even if it had had a name.

In more modern times armed men came to set up camp on the hill. They didn't come to hunt the wild game, but to use its commanding position to stop other forces from going through the valley down into the plain below.

In 1942 the Rising Sun flag of the Imperial Japanese Army was raised over a small encampment built on the crest of the hill. To these sons of the Rising Sun the hill had been known as Outpost 213, and being stationed there was considered a hardship tour. For the most part the Japanese troops spent their time tending their gardens and hunting to supplement their meager rations. Occasionally they fought the Bru and Rade tribesmen, commonly known as Montagnards, who still considered the valley to be their traditional hunting grounds. Mostly, however, their enemies were boredom and disease. When their war was over, the Japanese troops slung their arms upside down and marched into the plains below to await transport back to their war-shattered home islands.

A few years later the place became known as Point Nadine when it had been guarded by a small triangular fort manned by an understrength company of the French Foreign Legion. They died to a man in the fall of 1953 when they were hit by a regiment of Vietminh anxious to get to the open plain to the east.

True to their warrior's tradition the Legionnaires hadn't allowed the enemy to pass until the last round had been fired and the last Legionnaire had fallen. Their young French officer had died gallantly in the first hour of the attack, but the veteran Legionnaires, mostly ex-German soldiers, had fought on with no thought of retreat.

A dozen years after that a Special Forces CIDG Company—Civilian Irregular Defense Group—reclaimed the French fortifications, named the hill Camp 826 and used it as a patrol base for operations along the border. When they were challenged by a North Vietnamese Army unit trying to dislodge them, they didn't fight to the death. The American Army didn't follow the traditions of the Legion of Strangers—not even the Special Forces. Rather than die in place they had evacuated the camp and left the task of denying the North Vietnamese access to the plains to artillery and air strikes.

Now the Americans were back to reclaim the hill once more. This time it wouldn't be allowed to fall, because it was a key point in a string of Special Forces fighting camps being built along the border. No effort would be spared to create a fortress capable of withstanding anything short of a division assault. And the small hilltop would again bear a new name.

A tall, sun-bronzed man wearing a faded tiger suit uniform walked up to the bare crest of the hill and looked out at the jungle around him. A battered, sun-faded green beret of the U.S. Army's elite Special Forces sat on his close-cropped brown hair. Silver captain's bars were pinned on the yellow, red and black shield-shaped Fifth Group Special Forces flash sewn on the front of the beret. A red bomb-burst-shaped patch hanging from the button of the right breast pocket of his shirt showed a skull wearing a green beret with the legend A-410—Sat Cong below it. The words *Sat Cong* were Vietnamese for *Kill Communists*.

Captain Mike Reese's faded blue eyes swept over the terrain, imprinting it on his mind. According to his map, the hill was known as Dak Sang 1208, and it was going to be the new home of his unit, CIDG Company A-410, for the foreseeable future.

A few short weeks ago A-410 had been a Mike Force—Special Forces Mobile Strike Force—unit based in Ban Phoc on the Camobodian border in the IV Corps area of Operation. Under the command of B-40 in Can Tho they had worked in the area south of the Parrot's Beak in support of Special Forces operations interdicting NVA movements from across the border.

Now, however, A-410 had been transferred to CCC, Command and Control Central, one of the three clandestine MACV-SOG Special Operations Commands. Now they were a part of the war-within-the-war in Vietnam.

Everyone knew what the conventional forces were doing in Southeast Asia: the Army and Marine Infantry beat the jungle looking for the North Vietnamese, the Air Force flew over and dropped bombs on them and the Navy sailed along the coastline shelling them occasionally.

Most people even knew about the elite unconventional units operating in-country, the most renowned being the Army's famous Special Forces. The Green Berets had received a great deal of media attention for their efforts to turn the indigenous minority tribesmen of Vietnam into light infantry units who could fight the Vietcong and the North Vietnamese Army with their own guerrilla warfare tactics. Known as the CIDG program, this was one of the most successful military operations anywhere in Southeast Asia.

Less well known, but even more effective, were the Mike Force companies. These were specially trained and equipped CIDG units formed from the Nung Chinese, Montagnards or Cambodian populations of South Vietnam. Most of them were airborne-qualified, and they specialized in heliborne operations. The Mike Force was used as a ready-reaction force, ready to go anywhere in-country at a moment's notice to reinforce a CIDG camp, exploit a ground contact or to act as a lightly armed but highly mobile attack force. Of the five combat parachute drops that took place during the Vietnam War, four of them were conducted by Mike Force units.

Almost no one, however, knew about the secret war fought by MACV-SOG. This was the real war-within-the-war. These operations were so deeply classified that the name SOG was thought to stand for Studies and Observations Group, instead of Special Operations Group, to confuse even those high-ranking American military officers who didn't have a need to know what SOG really did for a living.

What MACV-SOG did for a living was kill the enemy. Its unofficial motto was Death Is Our Business—And Business Has Been Good.

MACV-SOG had been formed in January 1964 to oversee the clandestine military operations necessary to the success of the war. Unlike the widely publicized "conventional" unconventional war fought in South Vietnam by the Special Forces CIDG and Mike Force units, SOG's activities were known only by those who had a strict need to know. These missions included strategic reconnaissance, intelligence gathering, raiding the enemy's home bases, POW rescue, rescuing downed pilots and aircrew, training and controlling agents in North Vietnam, forming resistance groups, kidnapping or assassinating key enemy personnel, and sabotage missions. All such business was conducted outside the borders of South Vietnam. Burma, Cambodia, Laos, North Vietnam and the three southwestern provinces of Red China were also within SOG's area of operations.

Although its operations were supervised by MACV, SOG took its orders directly from the special assistant for counterinsurgency and special activities of the Joint Chiefs of Staff at the Pentagon. SOG operational personnel were drawn from the elite units of all services, but most were Army Special Forces personnel assigned to the Special Operations Augmentation unit of Fifth Group, U.S. Special Forces.

These men fought their secret battles deep in enemy territory, far from the highly publicized helicopter war televised on the six o'clock news. Not only was their war classified at the highest possible level, but also when they died, the where, how and why of their deaths was kept secret. Not even closest family members knew that their loved ones had fallen in Laos, Cambodia or North Vietnam on a SOG "black" operation.

Probably the most important of the SOG missions were the cross-border reconnaissances and intelligence-gathering operations in enemy territory known as Operation Shining Brass. With the political limitations that had been imposed upon the movements of the conventional American forces in Southeast Asia, normal military operations couldn't be conducted in the North Vietnamese sanctuaries in the officially neutral nations along South Vietnam's western border. But, if the U.S. Army couldn't take the war to the enemy, at least it had to know what they were doing in there. This mission was given to the MACV-SOG RTs, the recon teams.

These Shining Brass out-country recon missions were dangerous beyond any normal use of the word. The RTs were usually made up of only four to six men, one or two American SF and the rest Nungs or Cambodians. The teams were armed and outfitted with foreign equipment, wearing camouflage or specially made black NVA-style uniforms, carrying NVA rucksacks and often even enemy weapons. Just about the only thing that could identify them as an American unit were the small rolls of U.S. C-ration toilet paper they all carried.

If the North Vietnamese spotted the RTs at a distance, their outlines would appear familiar and they would pass for just another NVA or VC unit on the march. Even at closer range, if the American team members kept out of sight, the Vietnamese-speaking Nungs could easily pose as VC or NVA.

A vast array of support backed up the RTs—choppers on standby to extract them if they stepped into it, Tac Air fighter bombers to occupy the enemy while they got out, and high-flying communications aircraft so that they could maintain contact with headquarters and report their observations.

Part of the RTs' support team were the units known as Hatchet Forces. These were specially selected Mike Force units composed of five Americans and thirty CIDG who had been given the responsibility of handling missions too big for a six-man recon team to undertake such as interdicting and destroying NVA units moving into South Vietnam. It was also their job to exploit information sent back by the RTs. And, in the event that a recon team was cut off from all other help, their duty was to fight their way in and rescue them.

As a Special Forces Mike Force company, the men of A-410 had already seen a great deal of the war. They had bled in the jungles, and they had bled in the plains. They had fought both by day and by night, usually outnumbered and with little support to call on if they got into trouble. They were all seasoned veterans and thought they had seen everything the war could send their way, but they were wrong.

Now they would fight a different war, the SOG war. Now they were Hatchet Force.

REESE TURNED and motioned to a small group of men securing a small helicopter landing zone right outside the wire. One man detached himself from the group and double-timed up the gentle slope.

Where Reese was bayonet-trim, this man was stocky. His bronzed complexion, dark, straight hair and jet-black eyes marked his American Indian ancestry. Master Sergeant Ray Pierce was the operations sergeant of A-410 and Reese's right hand. A twenty-one-year infantry veteran, Pierce had won his first CIB, Combat Infantry Badge, in the frozen hills of Korea in 1951 and was now on his third tour with Fifth Group Special Forces in Vietnam.

"How long do you think it'll take us to be up and running here, Sarge?" Reese asked.

Pierce looked around with a professional eye. It wasn't the first time he'd been ordered to build a camp in the jungle. At least the location was suitable. Although the hill was small, it was high enough to dominate the surrounding area and give them good fields of fire in all directions. A well-graded dirt road led back down into the valley at their rear. It was a better place to make a stand than many he had seen in his long career as a professional soldier.

"If we get all the support SOG promised us," he said, "we should be okay in a week, eight days at the most." Pierce paused and smiled thinly. "But, as you and I both know, Captain, we're probably going to have to do most of it ourselves. The support we've been promised will probably turn out to be a chopper-load of sandbags and a case of plastic spoons."

Reese chuckled. He hadn't been through this as many times as Pierce, but he knew only too well not to trust promises made by people who worked in air-conditioned offices far from the realities of making war in the jungle.

"We'd better get them started, then, Sarge," he said. "We've got a lot of sandbags to fill."

"I'll get Torres on the horn, sir, and tell him to get the LT on his way."

2

June 28, Dak Sang, RVN

While a heavy gun team of UH-1C Huey Hog gunships circled protectively overhead, the first Huey slicks of Reese's troop lift touched down outside the wire. The first man off the lead chopper was First Lieutenant Jack Santelli, the XO, or executive officer.

Santelli was a wiry, dark-haired man whose dark eyes and olive skin indicated his Italian ancestry. He wore his tiger suit with authority, and his green beret was canted down and almost covered his right eye. He looked like a movie star version of a Special Forces officer, but the well-used CAR-15 in his hands was all business.

Santelli was an Italian kid straight from the Bronx, and not too many men from the big cities found their way into an organization that spent most of its time fighting in the jungles of Southeast Asia. But then Santelli wasn't your average New Yorker, either.

When he graduated from high school, Santelli immediately enlisted in the Army. After completing basic training and AIT, he was chosen to go on to Officers' Candidate School at Fort Benning.

He did well in OCS, and upon receiving his commission as an infantry second lieutenant, signed up for

Airborne training and Ranger School. After sewing the coveted Ranger tab on his uniform, he decided he wanted to add the famous green beret to his list of military accomplishments and was accepted at the John F. Kennedy Special Warfare School at Fort Bragg, North Carolina.

When he graduated from the Special Forces school, Santelli was shipped off to Vietnam and made the XO of A-410. But he quickly discovered that he liked field duty more than taking care of the day-to-day business of running an A-team. Fortunately their new assignment promised him lots of time in the woods.

"Who'd you bring with you?" Reese asked his XO.

Santelli jerked a thumb back at the troops off-loading the choppers. "I've got Vao and the two Nung platoons," he replied. "As well as Torres, Webb, Wilson and Kowalski."

Until Reese's new camp was completed the A-team had to leave enough people at the Ban Phoc camp to guard supplies and help the new A-team take over the base.

The other four A-team members checked in with Reese, and he gave them their assignments. Sergeant Antonio Torres, the radioman, had to set up a temporary command post in the center of the hill. Sergeant Larry Webb, the engineer, was to start laying out the camp's perimeters. Staff Sergeant Luther "Silk" Wilson was assigned to help Torres and set up his aid station in the CP. Sergeant First Class Gil Kowalski, the team's intelligence specialist, was Sergeant Pierce's backup in supervising the activities.

As soon as the Americans went about their tasks, an older Oriental approached Pierce and Santelli. *"Ni hoa, Dai Uy,"* the man said, coming to attention in front of Reese, greeting him in Nung Chinese, but using his Vietnamese rank title.

Reese smiled at seeing Ninh Le Vao, the Nung commander of his Mike Force. *"Ni hoa, Vao,"* he replied. "Are your people ready to go to work? We have *beaucoup* sandbags to fill before dark."

Vao smiled back. "Every Nung has his shovel today, *Dai Uy,* and they will dig like demons. I will see to that."

"They'd better. We're a long way from help if the Cong are out there watching us arrive."

"They are watching us," Vao stated flatly. "I can smell them."

Reese didn't bother to argue that point with the old jungle fighter. If Vao said the NVA were there, they were there. The Nung leader was in his late forties, and he had been fighting Communists longer than the young American officer had been alive. Every year of this long war was etched on his weathered face. Any Westerner who said they couldn't tell the age of an Oriental had never met Vao.

A veteran of the Chinese Nationalist Army, Vao had fought both the Japanese and Mao's Communists in World War II. Later he had joined up with the French in North Vietnam to fight against Ho Chi Minh's Communist Vietminh. Now, at an age when most soldiers had long since been retired, the wiry old Nung Chinese was still fighting Communists.

Turning around, Vao rattled off a long string of orders in the Nung dialect, and his troops scrambled to obey. Among the indigenous peoples involved in the Vietnam War, none were more fiercely anti-Communist and loyal to the cause of freedom than the Nung Chinese. Unlike the South Vietnamese who often played both sides of the conflict, or the Montagnards who sometimes just got fed up and went home to their wives and pigs, the Nungs were America's most efficient, faithful and trusted allies.

The Nungs had first come into Vietnam well over a thousand years earlier in the vanguard of the army of a Chinese general who had conquered the region for his emperor. When the original war was over, they had stayed behind in Vietnam and become farmers, but each time a new enemy appeared, they raised their dreaded black flags and took up arms again. Over the years they had gained a reputation as being the fiercest warriors in southeast Asia.

History had often witnessed the Nungs and the Vietnamese on opposite sides of a conflict and, in many ways, the Vietnam War was no different. The Vietnamese hated the Nungs for all the reasons one people dredge up to hate another and persecuted them whenever they could get away with it. For their part, the Nungs simply wanted to be left alone to live their lives, but if they were pushed around, they fought back. That was why they had flocked to join the American Special Forces SOG and CIDG mercenary programs. They were tired of being pushed around by both the North and the South Vietnamese. Their loyalty to the Americans was so well regarded that Special Forces CIDG camps had a Nung detachment to guard the U.S. cadre, and the elite SF Mobile Strike Force units, like Reese's company, were all Nung.

Within minutes there was a flurry of activity on the small hilltop. Sergeant Pierce and Webb marked off the outer perimeter and chose firing positions for the machine guns while right behind them the Nungs picked their fighting positions. As Vao had promised, every Nung had an entrenching tool, and before long the filled sandbags started piling up.

One of the first things the Nungs did was to dig in a pair of Browning M-2 .50-caliber heavy machine guns in the center of the hill. As far as modern infantry weapons went, the M-2 .50 caliber was an antique dating back to the end of the First World War, but there had never been a weapon as well loved as the old Ma Deuce. Despite several attempts to design a new heavy machine gun to replace it, she was still in the inventory doing what she did best—spitting out heavy-caliber slugs at a rate of five hundred rounds per minute.

Over the past fifty years the M-2 .50 caliber had been used in aircraft, on tanks, as an antiaircraft gun on ships and as a plain, hard-hitting infantry ground support weapon. In Korea they had even been mounted with telescopic sights and used as sniper rifles.

On battlefields worldwide, when Ma Deuce talked, it was best to listen up carefully. If anybody decided to mess with the camp before Reese got his defenses built, having Ma Deuce on the job might make all the difference in the world between counting bodies in the morning or being the ones who were counted.

Once the guns were set up and the sandbag parapets constructed, the Nungs started sacking the heavy ammunition cans for the guns. Even at the relatively low firing rate of only five hundred rounds per minute, Ma Deuce could burn through a lot of ammunition if she got pissed.

BY NIGHTFALL the camp was defendable, but just barely. The sandbagged fighting holes for the Nungs were dug, a double row of concertina wire was stretched out around the perimeter and the M-18A1 claymore command-detonated, antipersonnel mines were emplaced directly behind the wire. The engineers were due in the following day to start building proper bunkers and weapons positions, but if they got hit tonight, the foxholes would have to do.

Reese had set up his temporary command post in the center of the hill where his command bunker would be built when the engineers arrived. He and Torres were just finishing up a dinner of cold C-rations when Santelli walked up, his CAR-15 slung over his shoulder.

"We're about as ready as we're going to be, Captain," he said. "Vao's got everyone pumped up and they're standing tall."

"Good," Reese answered. "We can't afford to slack off here."

Santelli took a seat on a sandbag. "Did you get a chance to see yesterday's *Stars and Stripes?*"

"I was a little too busy trying to organize this monkey fuck," Reese commented dryly.

"Well," Santelli said, "it looks like the Marines have declared that they won the battle of Khe Sanh and they're starting to pull out. And, to celebrate the victory, the U.S. negotiators in Paris have offered to pull all of us out if the dinks will do the same."

Reese shook his head. "Fat chance of that," he said. "Since Johnson quit bombing the North, they don't have any reason to pull out. If anything, they're going to turn up the heat. Also, now that Johnson's given up the presidency and Westy's being kicked upstairs, the dinks are convinced they're winning this thing. There's just no fucking way they're going to back off now. They've got us by the short hairs and they know it."

"Maybe we'll get a new President in November who knows how to fight a war," Santelli said without real hope.

Reese snorted. "I wouldn't bet the farm on that one, LT. Don't you know that wars are real unpopular with politicians nowadays?"

Santelli laughed. "Maybe they should come over and talk to us for a while so they can find out how unpopular politicians are with us."

"Now you're really dreaming."

With darkness already fallen there was little for the A-team to do but to wait the night out. Pierce, Kowalski and Webb were down on the perimeter with the Nungs, leaving Wilson and Torres to share the radio watch. While Santelli took the first shift as officer of the guard, Reese tried to get some sleep, as the next day promised to be even busier. He was just drifting off when the distinctive thunking sound of 82 mm mortar rounds leaving the tubes echoed from the hills.

"Incoming!" someone shouted from the perimeter, but Reese was already in the bottom of his hole before the first mortar round hit.

"Welcome to Dak Sang, Captain!" Torres shouted over the crashing explosion.

Reese crouched even lower in the hole, swearing under his breath. Goddamn those bastards in MACV-SOG for sending them there. A second thunderous explosion lit up the night and sent dirt showering down onto the small CP. He scrambled over to Torres and reached for the radio handset. "Get me the CCC push!" he shouted as more mortar rounds detonated.

Torres switched the radio over to the frequency for Command and Control Central in Kontoum. "It's set!"

Reese keyed the mike. "Black Snake, Black Snake, this is Bent Talon Six, over."

"Black Snake, go."

"This is Talon Six. We are under attack by at least two tubes of 82 mortar."

"This is Snake. Roger, copy. I'll try to get some gunships to your location ASAP."

"Bent Talon, tell 'em to get a move on it. Out."

Suddenly the mortar fire cut off. Someone on the perimeter fired a jack-off flare, and when the small illumination flare popped over the hill, the flickering yellowish light revealed a dozen dark shapes scrambling up the east side of the hill.

A storm of small-arms fire broke out along that side of the perimeter, and more jack-off flares were fired to keep the attacking NVA illuminated. From the center of the camp the two .50s opened up, adding their characteristic slow-paced, heavy, chunking fire to the defense. Ma Deuce was speaking again.

Only halfway up the hill the enemy was caught out in the open with nowhere to hide. The only thing they could do was to run back down for the cover of the jungle. The Nungs fired as long as they had moving targets, and few of the NVA reached the protection of the tree line.

As soon as the firing tapered off, Santelli ran up to the CP. In the flickering light of the flares Reese saw that he was grinning. "No sweat, Captain. It was just a ground probe trying to see if we were awake. There were about ten or twelve, but we got most of them before they could get back down the hill."

"Anyone get hurt?"

"We've got a couple of minor frag wounds, but nothing needing Dust-off."

Reese turned to Torres. "Report six rounds of 82 and a squad-size ground probe, but no serious casualties. And have them cancel the gunships. I think it's over for the night, but ask them to stay on standby just in case."

3

June 29, MACV-SOG Headquarters, Tan Son Nhut

CIA agent Dick Clifford was at his desk in his second-story office in the MACV-SOG Headquarters building at the edge of sprawling Tan Son Nhut Air Force Base. As usual he was at work early and had just poured the first of the innumerable cups of coffee he would drink before the day was over. He sipped the coffee as he went through the night's messages in his in box.

The first item he came to was the report from Command and Control Central in Kontoum about the attack on the new camp at Dak Sang during the night. He knew Mike Reese and the men of A-410. He had worked with them the previous month when they were sent into the Parrot's Beak on a high-priority SOG mission. In fact, he was the man who had put the mission together and, indirectly, he was responsible for their deployment to Dak Sang to build the new border camp.

He put the report down and stared out of his window to watch the sun rise over the massive air base complex on the outskirts of Saigon. At the end of the main runway three camouflaged F-4 Phantom fighter bombers cracked their afterburners as they started down the runway, their wings heavy with olive drab high-explosive eggs. Help was on the way to someone this morning. The aircraft might even be heading north to provide A-410 with air support. Someone had better give Reese a hand. It looked as though they had stepped into a real hornet's nest, and even though that was the fortunes of war, Clifford felt responsible.

The CIA man hunched his tall, thin frame over the desk. His close-cropped black hair and dark eyes accentuated the paleness of his skin. His lack of an in-country tan told of a life lived mostly inside the dim corridors of the MACV-SOG building. While most of the personnel in SOG were military, a large number of CIA and DIA agents as well as other civilians also worked within the secret organization.

The civilians were mostly involved with the administrative and logistical end of running SOG's clandestine operations, but Clifford worked for the Ground Studies operations section and evaluated intelligence information, specifically information on enemy forces gathered by the SOG RTs, the Air Force spy planes and the far-flung CIA field agent network.

Clifford was typical of many of the CIA men of his generation. He came from a wealthy east coast family and had majored in foreign relations at Georgetown University, planning to go into the diplomatic service. Kennedy's presidency, however, changed his plans. Like so many young Americans in college at that time, he, too, got caught up in the youthful President's stirring "Ask Not What Your Country Can Do for You" inaugural speech.

But after the Cuban missile crisis, the building of the Berlin Wall, the Bay of Pigs fiasco and the youthful President Kennedy's assassination, he realized the best thing he could do for his country was to help guard her from communism. A military career wasn't something he had ever considered, but the life of a CIA agent appealed to him.

Clifford went through extensive training at the CIA's headquarters in Langley, Virginia, at the infamous "farm," and went on to specialize in intelligence analysis and evaluation. Although he had wanted an assignment in Europe, preferably West Berlin, he was sent to Vietnam and ended up working at MACV-SOG Headquarters. It wasn't quite the dashing, cloak-and-dagger Company job he had dreamed about, but he had to admit it had its moments, particularly at times like this when he had to see his boss and give him bad news.

Clifford answered to Colonel Stewart A. Marshall, the MACV-SOG Ground Studies operations officer. Where most of the SOG military personnel were free-thinking, bomb-throwing radicals who loved the strange and wild life of clandestine unconventional operations, Marshall was a throwback to a much earlier era when the infantry wore pretty red coats and advanced in neat, straight lines. Hitting the beaches at Normandy was about as close as he could come to new methods of warfare, and he was totally out of place in SOG's war in the jungles of Southeast Asia.

Marshall was also uncomfortable dealing with the CIA, which was why Clifford dreaded each time he had to go into the crusty old bastard's office with bad news. Marshall automatically blamed the Company in general and Clifford in particular when anything went wrong with an operation. As far as the colonel was concerned, spies were about as welcome in his Army as working whores were in a nunnery. He felt that it wasn't gentlemanly to spy on the enemy, and he was even skeptical of the need for intelligence gathering by the RTs.

Clifford thought that having a man like Marshall in charge of SOG operations was a stupid way to run a war, but many things about the war in Vietnam were no better.

He drained the last of his coffee and picked up the report. The morning had hardly started, but already he could tell he was going to have a lousy day.

He knocked on the door at the end of the hall and waited until Marshall called out. Even though Clifford wasn't in the military, the colonel liked the civilian personnel on his staff to halt at the military regulation three paces in front of his oak desk and stand at attention until he offered them a seat.

"Sir," Clifford said after he assumed the position, "the new Hatchet Force camp at Dak Sang is already attracting attention from the NVA. They got hit last night with mortar fire and ground probes."

"That's Reese's camp, right?" Marshall asked.

"Yes, sir."

"Have a seat."

Marshall was a soldier of the old school. A tanker by trade, he had roamed over Europe as a second lieutenant in the command hatch of an M-4 Sherman tank with an armored battalion in Patton's Third Army. Later, in Korea, he had commanded a company of M-46 Pershing tanks against the Russian-built

T-34 tanks of the North Koreans. Marshall understood fire and maneuver, particularly when it came to deploying armored forces, but he didn't understand the daily realities of the clandestine war they were engaged in.

Only a whim of the capricious gods of war could have given a tanker like Marshall an assignment as the operations officer for the dirtiest war being fought in Nam—the MACV-SOG clandestine operations. But in a country covered with jungle and rice paddies, there wasn't much use for tankers, and he had to do something to earn his paycheck.

"Let's see it," Marshall said, reaching for the radio message.

Clifford handed the colonel the report from CCC. Marshall slowly smiled as he read over the message. The half-formed plan he kept stored in the back of his mind was coming into sharper focus. He had originally chosen Reese's unit for this Hatchet Force assignment as a punishment because the young SF officer had pissed him off. But now it was beginning to look as if Reese might be useful to Marshall's plans, and if that was how the cards were dealt, he had to make sure the SF captain stayed alive long enough.

"When are the combat engineers due to arrive there?"

"They're due in early this morning, sir," Clifford answered.

Marshall grunted. "Good. Keep on them and make sure they have every last damn thing they think they need. I don't want to hear that they're running into problems. Dak Sang has got to be up and running as soon as humanly possible.''

''Yes, sir.''

''Get back to Reese and tell him to hang in there,'' Marshall added. ''Also, go through CCC and get artillery and air support laid on ASAP. I don't want Reese to get pushed out of there.''

''Yes, sir.''

''And I want a report on everything this afternoon before I go home.''

''Yes, sir.''

On his way back to his office Clifford mulled over Marshall's reaction. For one thing, he hadn't blamed Clifford for not having foretold the attack. He hadn't even blamed Reese for being attacked. And he had actually smiled when he read the report.

Something was wrong here, but the CIA agent didn't have any idea what it was. The only thing he knew was that someone was in for a hard time. Every time Colonel Marshall smiled like that, someone was going to find himself in deep shit.

IN DOWNTOWN SAIGON Laura Winthrop again caught herself staring out her second-story window in the United Press International building. She snapped her blue eyes back to her well-worn typewriter with the sticking *E* key, but she wasn't able to find the right words to finish her story on the new orphanage under construction outside Ben Hoa for Vietnamese children recently orphaned by the Tet Offensive.

It wasn't really a bad story. It was oozing with the kind of human interest slant that would play well with middle America, but it wasn't what she had busted her ass in Columbia University's School of Journalism to write about. She had come to Vietnam to write about the war, not to do fluff pieces from a "woman's angle." She wanted to write about something with more meat in it, specifically the broken, bleeding meat of the men and women who had been caught up in the seemingly endless, useless war.

Laura ran her fingers through her long blond hair and rubbed the back of her neck. Most male journalists followed the Hemingway school of war correspondence and tried to emulate their hero. But Laura's literary heroes were Martha Gellhorn, Hemingway's third wife and a brilliant war correspondent in her own right, and the French female journalist who had died in an ambush covering a combat patrol with the Marines.

As it was, she had been in Vietnam for six months, and the fighting she had seen had been in Saigon during Tet. And even that she had been forced to watch from a safe distance. Every time she had come up with a story idea that would let her cover the real war, it had been turned down by her editor.

As she had done several times a day for the past few weeks, her mind flashed back to her initial conversation with Mike Reese the night she had met him in the dining room of the Continental Palace Hotel in Saigon. When she told him her view of the war, he had invited her to visit him and see a part of the war that was successful—the Special Forces war. At first she hadn't taken his offer seriously, but after her second and much more intimate meeting with Reese, she had reconsidered.

She definitely wanted to take him up on his offer, but her visit had been sidetracked by several busy work assignments. The human interest scene in Saigon had heated up as the American command feverishly tried to take the American public's mind off the fact that they had screwed up again and the enemy was close enough to the South Vietnamese capital to launch another surprise attack, the one the papers were calling Mini-Tet.

But if she couldn't get assigned to cover the war, maybe she could get some time off and spend the time in-country researching what she wanted to write about. Then, when she had the story in hand, she could try to persuade her editor to send it out.

Now that she knew what she was going to do she turned back to her typewriter. Her hands flew over the keys, stopping only to unstick the *E* key each time it hung up. The only advantage she had ever seen to being a female reporter was that at least she had been taught how to type in high school. Most of the men she worked with usually typed with only two or three fingers.

Rolling the last page out of the typewriter, she added it to the rest of the story and, after checking it over briefly, headed for her editor's office. As always Vince Phillips was at his desk. After inviting her into his office, Phillips looked over Laura's orphanage story while she talked. It wasn't a bad story, but it wasn't anything to rave about, either. But then what had he expected? It was a nothing story to begin with, and Phillips had Laura working for him only because the home office had insisted he have a woman on his staff.

Several women had applied for the job, some of them old-timers at the business, but he had chosen Laura over the more experienced ones. He hadn't chosen her for her brilliant writing skills, her dogged determination to do an outstanding job or even for her keen insight into the human condition. Phillips had chosen her for her magnificent body, and for the faint possibility that he might somehow be able to talk her into going to bed.

So far, however, bedding Laura had remained only a fantasy that he played out each time he made his weekly visits to the Vietnamese whores. But, try as he might, he just couldn't pretend that the skinny, dark-haired Vietnamese girls he paid for were the lush-figured, long-haired blond reporter with the deep blue eyes and full bosom.

As far as he was concerned, if he couldn't get her, she might as well get out of the office so that he didn't have to look at her all the time.

"Sure," he said when she got to her request for a couple of weeks off. "Take some time off."

"Thanks a lot, Vince," she said as she stood to leave.

"No sweat," he replied, his eyes following the sway of her hips as she walked out. He slowly shook his head as he went back to his work. Christ, what a body!

4

June 29, Dak Sang, RVN

Shortly after 0800 that morning the thundering beat of helicopter rotors echoed throughout the valley. A flight of three twin-rotor CH-47 Chinook heavy-lift choppers escorted by a Light Gun team of three Huey Hogs appeared from the east. As they drew closer, Reese saw that two of the shithooks had what appeared to be small bulldozers sling-loaded underneath them. It looked as though SOG really was serious about getting this camp built. Usually troops armed with entrenching tools were about all a commander could expect in the line of earth-moving equipment at a new campsite. This would make the bunker-building chores almost easy.

The flight leader quickly got into radio contact with the A-team, and smoke grenades were popped to guide the choppers in for a landing. As the Huey gunships circled overhead, the first of the Chinooks dropped out of the sky. Even though the Nungs were as familiar with helicopters as any Air Cav trooper, everyone stopped what they were doing to watch the big shithooks land. There was something about a chopper the size of a bus hanging motionless in the sky that made a man look up.

The blast of the shithook's twin rotors raised a storm of red dirt as it gingerly touched down on all four of its landing gear. The pilot kept the rotors turning as he dropped the rear ramp, and the men inside hurried to off-load the cargo. The hilltop could only accommodate two of the huge helicopters at the same time.

One man detached himself from the group and, seeing Reese standing by his temporary CP, walked over to him and stuck his hand out. "I'm Captain Jack Hemmings, combat engineer. I understand you want us to build you a camp."

Reese grinned and shook his hand. "Mike Reese, and you've come to the right place."

Hemmings took a quick look around. "I've seen worse places to do it," he said, shifting his cigar to the other side of his mouth.

"So have I," Reese agreed. "As soon as we get some bunkers built, we should be in pretty good shape."

"What kind of bunkers are we talking about here?"

"We're only six klicks from the fence, so we'll need something with good overhead cover to stand up against artillery fire."

The engineer chomped on his cigar. "How about bunkers built with six-by-six timbers, PSP roofs and all the fucking sandbags in the world?"

Reese grinned. "That sounds about right."

"Where do you want 'em?"

Reese took the sketch map out of the side pocket of his tiger suit pants. "I want the main gate over on the east side—" he pointed out the location "—and then a circular perimeter with about twenty bunkers spaced evenly around the circle should about do it for us.''

The engineer studied the map for a moment. "Where do you want your CP?"

"Right here in the middle," Reese answered. "And I'd like to have it put in first so I can set up my commo gear as soon as possible."

"Can do."

Hemmings turned around and, spotting one of his men supervising the unloading of the shithooks, bellowed, "Sergeant Gilmore! Over here!"

Gilmore dropped what he was doing and double-timed over to his officer. The sergeant had taken his fatigue jacket off, but when he got closer, Reese saw that sergeant first class stripes were tattooed on his biceps. Talk about someone who took his work seriously!

"Yes, sir."

"This man—" Hemmings jerked a thumb at Reese "—wants a CP bunker built ASAP, a bombproof bunker."

Gilmore worked a wad of chewing tobacco in his mouth and spit a stream of juice off to the side. "Where do you want it, sir?"

Once he had pointed out the locations of the main positions for his camp, Reese turned the job over to the professionals and went back to planning the camp's defense.

While Reese worked on his defense plans, Torres was busy on his radio calling in preplanned artillery concentrations to the 155 mm howitzer battery that had been assigned to support the camp. By preplanning the targets for the big guns, he wouldn't have to waste precious time registering the guns while under attack. The artillery could just shoot on the coordinates that had already been plotted and adjust the fire from them.

"Sir, I'm done here," the RTO told Reese. "I've got eight preplanned concentrations, including a Firecracker dinks-in-the-wire shot."

Firecracker artillery rounds were shells that contained many small round bomblets instead of just one large explosive charge. The shells exploded in the air above the target and rained the bomblets down on the enemy. This was particularly useful in a defensive situation where the friendlies were down in their holes and the enemy was storming the wire. That was exactly the sort of situation they could expect if they got hit again before the construction was completed.

"That sounds about right," Reese answered. "But let's hope we don't have to use the Firecrackers."

"You've got that shit right, sir," Torres replied.

LAURA WINTHROP WAS more than ready to take Mike Reese up on his offer to show her the real war, but she was having a difficult time learning his exact whereabouts. So far all she had learned was that he was apparently still somewhere in-country.

When she put through a land line call to his last known address, the Special Forces camp at Ban Phoc, she had simply been told that he was no longer there. When she asked for his new location, she had been given the runaround. She remembered that he had mentioned working for the SF headquarters in Can

Tho, but when she contacted them, the only word she got was that his unit had been transferred. Further inquiries only yielded more of the old runaround. It was beginning to look as though Reese had disappeared from the face of the planet. Either that or he had been sucked into the void of the "other war" of Special Forces operations.

Like everyone else in Vietnam, Laura knew about the more publicized activities of Special Forces, the "super soldiers" of the war, and had figured out that most of it was pure hype. But after meeting Reese and hearing what he had to say, she had become interested in Special Forces operations and had talked to some of the old Asian hands at the office about what the SF was really all about.

Some of them had been openly contemptuous of the popular John Wayne image of the Special Forces. But a few of the older men had smiled secretly and hinted at things she had never heard of: huge CIA-financed armies in Laos led by SF officers, raids into North Vietnam, assassinations, books of gold sheets used to pay tribesmen, and booby-trapped enemy ammunition supplies. It sounded like something straight out of a James Bond novel, but she sensed there was something behind the tall tales. The more she tried unsuccessfully to find Mike Reese, the more she believed he had gotten caught up in this cloak-and-dagger side of the war.

The search for Reese was becoming a mystery, and Laura loved mysteries. The first thing she did to try to solve this one was to fall back on a woman's most effective weapon—her femininity.

Unlike many beautiful women, Laura didn't consider herself as such. She was, however, well aware of the effect she had on certain men. She knew, for instance, that her editor went into a hormonal overload whenever he was around her. She also knew how to use this effect to her advantage when she had to, and, it looked as though it was going to be one of those times.

There was one place in Vietnam that had to keep track of everyone's whereabouts at all times—MACV's personnel office, the G-1. It was easy enough for her to locate the officer who kept the records for the Special Forces men in Vietnam. The captain was quite willing to do anything to help her until he opened Reese's field 201-file and saw he was assigned to MACV-SOG. Suddenly he wasn't quite so helpful.

"I'm sorry, Miss Winthrop," he said seriously, closing the file folder. "But I can't give you any information about Captain Reese."

Laura had always been able to cry on command, and now she let the tears form in the corner of her eyes.

"But I have to get in contact with him," she said with a little catch in her voice. She leaned even closer as the tears slid down her cheeks. "You see, I'm pregnant and I really have to talk to him. My parents, they're—" She choked back a sob.

The captain sat back in his chair, a storm of emotions flashing across his face—fear that he'd find his ass in a serious crack if he told her where Reese was, anger at a man who would get such a beautiful woman into a predicament like that, and lust when he thought about the act of getting her pregnant. The lust and anger won out over the fear.

"Look," he said, lowering his voice. "I can't tell you where he is, and I can't even tell you the reason why. But if you can find some way to travel to a place called Dak Sang up in II Corps, you might find out where he is."

Laura smiled when she walked out of the MACV Headquarters building. She was quite pleased with her performance, and if any of this ever got back to Reese she was sure she could smooth things over with him. What counted at the moment was that she finally had a name.

The name Dak Sang, however, proved to be meaningless. Even when she consulted her maps they showed her nothing. She asked around, and no one had ever heard of it. Eventually she learned that the name sounded more Laotian than Vietnamese. So rather than give up, Laura pulled out all the stops. She finally had a name, and by God she was going to find the place that went with the name if it took her the rest of the month.

When all else failed, Laura let her fingers do the walking through the USARV phone book that listed the land line connections in-country. She found what she was looking for in less than fifteen minutes: Lynx 2418, the phone number of the Sixty-sixth Engineer Company—Topographic—in Long Binh. If anyone would know where Dak Sang was, it would be the Army's mapmakers.

Rather than waste time trying to call and risk being put off, Laura decided on the personal approach.

Combing her hair down and putting on a thin silk blouse, she caught a ride out to Long Binh. The small mapmaking unit was easy to find, and getting what she wanted proved even easier. She only had to lean over the desk when she showed the young engineer lieutenant her press card.

The instant the lieutenant's eyes focused on the V-neck of her blouse, he became the most helpful man in the world. He took her arm and led her back into the map room. He briefly referred to the Vietnam gazette, and then, opening a drawer, pulled out a 1/12500 topographic map sheet. A second later his finger pointed to a spot in the jungle.

There it was—Dak Sang 1208, a small hill in a valley along the border close to where the corners of Laos and Cambodia came together. What the hell was Reese doing up there? Laura wondered. Whatever it was, though, she was going to find out.

"Can I get a copy of that map?" she asked.

"Sure," the topographer said eagerly as he started folding the map. "You can have this one."

Armed with the map, Laura went back to her Saigon apartment to pack her bag for a long trip.

BY NIGHTFALL that evening the small hill at Dak Sang had been totally transformed. It wasn't a finished camp yet, but it was quickly coming along. The perimeter had been scraped level and proper wire barriers put up. The primary machine-gun bunkers had been started and most of the firing positions dug out. Buried ammo bunkers had been built, but the rest of the supplies were still out in the open.

Reese's CP bunker had been already dug in. Four of the steel conex containers the engineers had brought full of supplies had been buried in the ground in a cruciform. The eighteen-by-eighteen-foot-square area in the center of the cross had been floored with PSP landing-strip mat laid over a timber floor. Six-by-six timber uprights supported a low roof also built with timbers. The next morning two layers of PSP with a layer of sandbags in the middle would be placed over the entire complex as a roof. Three or four more layers of sandbags would go over that with a final top layer of PSP to complete the bunker's overhead cover.

When it was done, Reese's CP would be as close to bombproof as it could be without pouring six feet of concrete over it. Until then, though, the bunker was open to the night sky. As he moved his radios and aid station inside the unfinished bunker, Reese hoped the NVA would give them the night off before they launched another mortar attack.

5

June 30, Dak Sang, RVN

Laura sat in the back of the Huey slick as it flew over the densely wooded mountains. She had been in the air for over an hour, and the constant vibration of the chopper's rotor had thoroughly numbed her entire body. She didn't see how the chopper crews could endure it for hours, but she realized that after a while one could get used to anything.

That was the primary reason she had resorted to every trick in the book to get on a chopper heading into the unknown. She hadn't wanted to get too comfortable writing stories about orphanages. It hadn't been easy to get this chopper ride, and she still wasn't completely sure she was going to the right place. But if the pilot was taking her to the Dak Sang he knew about, she figured she had a better than even chance of finding Mike Reese and getting her story.

Even if it was the wrong place and she had to spend the night among strangers, it could prove to be a better story than the ones she had been writing. But she had an inner certainty that she would find Reese somewhere before she was done. After all, she had gone to a lot of trouble to get this far....

AFTER SHE HAD LEFT SAIGON on an early-morning C-130 flight out of Tan Son Nhut, Laura's first stop had been in the beautiful town of Nha Trang on the South China Sea. Not only was Nha Trang the home of Fifth Group Special Forces headquarters, it also had the palatial MACV press camp, the home away from home for the Vietnam press corps.

Laura hadn't been to Nha Trang before, but she had heard the war stories about the press camp from the male journalists. In between guided tours of the battlefields and firebases in the jungle, the men would stop in at the press camp for several days each week to do their laundry and eat hot meals before they headed back out on another guided tour to cover the war.

Nha Trang was situated along a gently curving bay on the eastern side of a spit of land formed by the mouth of the Cua Be River. Inland, on the other side of the river, the verdant green of the jungle-covered Dong Bo Mountains formed a perfect backdrop for the clear blue water and gleaming sand of the postcard-pretty bay. Modern hotels and French colonial villas faced a broad beachfront boulevard lined with palm trees. Because of the constant breezes off the South China Sea, the climate was milder and considerably cooler than just a few miles inland.

Nha Trang was a tropical paradise, and the MACV press camp was an air-conditioned palace a mere five-minute walk away from the beach. Nha Trang was also considered to have the best-looking prostitutes in Vietnam, and from what Laura had heard, they were quite a draw.

However, Laura wasn't in town to get drunk, get laid or lie on the beach and work on her tan. Nha Trang was simply the best place to use as a base camp while she tried to find a way to get to Dak Sang. And, if she was staying in Nha Trang, she might as well make use of the press camp's facilities. She figured the camp's PIO, the public information officer, might prove very helpful to her mission.

The press camp PIO, a young first lieutenant, was more than willing to help the blond reporter, but he couldn't come up with any information about a Special Forces camp at Dak Sang. Everyone he talked to claimed not to know anything about a camp there. Even the Special Forces headquarters said they hadn't had anyone in Dak Sang since the last CDIG camp had been overrun well over a year before.

By midafternoon it was obvious to Laura that she was getting the old military runaround yet again. The personnel officer at MACV wouldn't have given her the name of a camp that didn't exist. He had been much too taken by her cover story. As far as she was concerned, if Special Forces headquarters was claiming they didn't have any people there, they had to be covering something up. It was the only answer that made any sense to her.

"I'm really sorry, Miss Winthrop," the PIO said, shaking his head. "I've never had this much trouble setting up an interview before. Are you sure you've got the right place?"

Laura nodded. "Yes, I've got the right place. He's at Dak Sang." She thought for a moment. "Can you find out who flies the resupply missions to the SF camps around here?''

"Sure thing." The PIO thumbed through a roster of the II Corps units and their missions. "That's the 281st Helicopter Company, and they're right here in Nha Trang."

"Can you get me a ride over there?"

"No sweat."

Finally it was her UPI press card that did the trick. After a quick jeep ride over to the operations shack of the 281st Helicopter Company on the other side of the air base, she simply showed her press card and asked if she could catch a lift to Dak Sang. The flight operations sergeant figured that if the lady reporter wanted to go to Dak Sang, she had business there and signed her up for the evening administration run.

Because Marshall was keeping such a tight lid on his plans for Dak Sang, no one had thought to tell the sergeant or his superiors that the camp was off-limits to reporters, even good-looking blond ones.

THE COPILOT TURNED around in his seat. "There it is, Miss Winthrop," he said, pointing through the canopy. "Dak Sang."

Laura unbuckled her seat belt and moved up behind him for a better look, but what she saw wasn't very impressive. In the dying light of the afternoon sun the camp was a raw red earth scar atop a small hill in the middle of a valley. She could barely make out the outlines of the perimeter, but she saw the stacks of supplies and what looked like a couple of vehicles. It was a very small place to have generated so much secrecy, and she wondered just exactly what Reese was doing there.

Since she wasn't wearing a flight helmet plugged into the Huey's intercom, she couldn't hear the radio communication between the pilot and the camp on the ground as the chopper circled the hill. She did see a smoke grenade burst into life in the center of the hill, sending a billowing column of purple smoke into the air.

The pilot made a final pass over the camp to line up with the wind and flared out for a landing next to the smoke grenade. "Can you wait for a minute?" she yelled at the pilot over the whine of the turbine. "I have to make sure I'm at the right place."

"I can give you a minute," he replied, glancing down at his watch. "But I've got a tight schedule."

Grabbing her bag, she stepped out onto the ground and looked around for Reese. A man broke away from a small group and walked toward her. As he got closer, she saw it was Reese. "Mike!" she called out.

"Laura!" Reese was stunned. "What in hell are you doing here?"

"Aren't you glad to see me?" she asked, her eyes challenging him. "You said I should come and see you sometime."

"Oh, sweet Jesus."

It was the first time Laura had seen the young Special Forces captain on the job. The two other times they had met in Saigon he had been dressed in clean, starched fatigues and polished boots. Right now he looked like something out of a Robert Capa snapshot of battle-weary troops just pulled off the front lines.

He was unshaven, and his normally sparkling, faded blue eyes showed the strain of the past couple of days. His faded tiger suit was dirty and sweat-stained, and even the green beret he usually wore so proudly looked limp and misshapen.

This was a Mike Reese she had never seen before. He wasn't the cool, suave, delightful man she had invited into her bed a month ago, and he wasn't at all pleased to see her. He was about as suave as a baseball bat up alongside the head. But, instead of diminishing his appeal, seeing him this way made him even more interesting.

"I'm here to take you up on your offer to let me see your side of the war," she told him.

He looked away for an instant and seemed to bite back an angry retort. "Look, Laura," he said when he turned back, "I know I told you to come see me, but this isn't the best place in the world for you to be right now. We've got dinks all around us and..." He paused and leaned closer to her. "Just how in hell did you find us, anyway? This is supposed to be a classified operation. Highly classified."

Not even giving her time to answer, he turned back to the chopper and gave the pilot a "cut the engines" signal by drawing his finger across his throat. The pilot didn't respond to Reese's signal. Instead, he tapped his watch and jerked his thumb up into the sky before pulling pitch to his spinning rotor blades. In a flurry of red dust the Huey rose into the air, pivoted in a hover and took off to the east.

"Oh, shit!" Reese muttered wearily. "Marshall's going to have my ass for this."

"Who's this Marshall guy?" she asked, catching the note of concern in Reese's voice and scenting a story behind it.

Now his face turned even grimmer. "Laura," he said urgently, "I shouldn't have said that. Forget you ever heard that name."

"Why?"

He gripped her arm. "Look, I mean it. You can't know that name, and it would be dangerous for you if you ever tried to find out who he is. Please," he pleaded, "promise me you'll forget all about it."

"Sure," she said, lying through her teeth. "I've forgotten it already. Now how about that story you promised me?"

Reese shook his head slowly. He should have known better than to get involved with a reporter. "Have you eaten?"

"I could use a bite," she admitted.

"I can't offer you much except Cs," he said, leading her back to his CP. "Our mess hall isn't set up yet."

"That'll be fine." She smiled. "In fact, it'll be a first for me."

Reese looked stunned. "You've never eaten C-rations? I thought even civilians in-country had a case stashed under their bed for midnight snacking."

"Not me."

"You're in for a real treat."

Reese led Laura over to his half-built CP bunker. The engineers had knocked off work for the night, but he had already moved his commo center inside, and Wilson was setting up his aid station. The roof wasn't on yet, so he had stretched several ponchos over the timbers to keep the light from showing.

With the unerring instinct of field troops throughout history, every man in Dak Sang quickly became aware that there was a woman in the camp. By the time they reached the CP, the A-team and the engineer officers had started filtering over to see who she was and what was going on.

Reese made the introductions, and Laura made small talk with the men for a few minutes. Sergeant Pierce pulled Reese aside and spoke quietly. "How in hell did she get up here, sir? SOG's going to shit bricks when they find out about this. We can't have reporters snooping around."

"I know," Reese said, rubbing the back of his neck. "And I'm putting her on the first chopper I can get in here tomorrow morning."

"I hope to hell the colonel doesn't find out about this."

"So do I, Sarge," Reese replied. "But that's what I get for talking to reporters."

6

June 30, Dak Sang

After the curious troops met Laura and went back to their own business, Reese took the reporter down inside the command bunker for the dinner he had promised her. Torres was standing watch over his radios, and Reese had him break open a fresh ration box to get something decent for Laura to eat. All that would be left from the boxes the men had already pawed through would be turkey loaf or ham and lima beans, and he didn't want to inflict either one of them on her for her first C-rats dining experience.

The radioman came back with a choice of entrée—a can of beanie weenies, one of chicken and noodles and a third of pork and beans. For side dishes he had provided the real C-ration delicacies: pound cake, fruit cocktail and hickory-smoked cheese with crackers.

She wisely chose the chicken and noodles, and Reese opened the cans for her with the P-38 can opener he carried attached to his dog-tag chain. He opened the accessory pack that came in the meal box for her, and she was amazed to see what it contained: coffee, powdered creamer, sugar, salt, gum, matches, cigarettes and toilet paper.

"I'd put that TP and coffee in your pocket if I were you," he said. "Those are real necessities in the field, and they're usually hard to come by."

"This isn't too bad," Laura said after she cautiously took a bite of the cold chicken and noodles. "But it's a little bland."

Torres reached into his rucksack and pulled out a bottle of Tabasco sauce. "Here," he offered, "this spices it up a little."

"No, thanks," she replied. "I think I'll take it straight."

Torres looked over and shuddered when he saw what Reese was eating for his own dinner. "How can you stand to eat those H and MFs, Captain?"

Reese smiled. "I love 'em. My mom used to cook them all the time and I never could get enough."

"What are H and MFs?" Laura asked.

Both men burst out laughing.

"What's funny?"

"You tell her, Captain."

"Well," Reese said with a broad grin, "H and MFs is troop slang for ham and limas."

"So? What does it mean?"

"It stands for ham and mater fornicators."

Laura caught on and laughed. "I take it they're not a real popular item with the troops."

"You got that right, ma'am," Torres said. "Most guys'll go hungry rather than have to eat them."

"That bad?"

Torres grimaced. "Believe me."

Reese looked up from his empty can. "They're better than turkey loaf."

Torres laughed. "Dog shit's better than turkey loaf, sir." The radioman immediately glanced over at Laura. "Sorry 'bout that, ma'am."

Laura smiled. "I've heard that word before. In fact, I've even been known to use it myself."

"Would you like some coffee?" Reese asked her.

"Please."

Reese tore off a small chunk of C-4 plastic explosive from a block he carried in his rucksack, dropped it into an empty ration can and lit it with a match to heat a canteen cup of water for hot coffee. When the water was hot, Laura saw that Reese was spooning instant coffee into the cup instead of using the C-ration coffee packets.

"You're cheating," she said. "That's PX coffee."

Reese grinned as he poured half the coffee into a second cup and handed it to her. "I might be stuck way the hell out in the ass end of the world, but I'm not completely stupid. That C-rat coffee's only for emergencies. No one drinks that shit unless they have to."

"Okay," she said, sipping the hot coffee. "Now how about my story?"

"What do you want to know?"

"I want to hear all about how you guys are winning the war."

Reese looked her straight in the eye. "I'm not really sure we're winning the war in this particular part of the country right now. When I gave you the invitation to visit me, I had something I could show you, but we left that back at Ban Phoc."

"What are you doing up here, anyway?"

"I can't tell you that," he said, his voice tightly controlled. "I really can't."

"And why doesn't anyone know you're up here?"

"I can't tell you that, either."

"What can you tell me?"

"Basically nothing," Reese admitted. "I'm sorry, but that's just the way it is."

"So you're telling me there's no story here?"

"I'm afraid that's about it. I'm sorry, but that's how it has to be. Like I said earlier, this is a classified operation, and it would be my head if I said anything about it."

He leaned closer to her, his face intense. "My best recommendation is that you just forget all about us. In fact, if I were you, I wouldn't even tell your friends you came up here to see me."

Laura was frightened by the intensity in his voice. She had never seen him this serious about anything.

"If you want to write about SF," he said, "I can give you the names of several guys in the Mike Force who'd love to show you their camps."

"And their etchings," she added dryly.

Reese laughed and glanced at his watch. "It's getting late, and I've got to make sure we're ready for the evening's activities. You'd better be thinking about getting a little sleep. You'll be getting up pretty early in the morning."

Laura checked her own watch and saw that it was only a little after nine. Late nights certainly had a different definition in the jungle. Even with the curfew in Saigon, as far as she was concerned, the evening was just beginning. But Reese obviously wanted to go about doing whatever it was he did at night here, and since he wasn't going to give her a story, there was little else for her to do.

"Okay," she said. "Where's the guest room?"

Reese laughed. "The sleeping arrangements are pretty primitive around here. All I can offer you is my air mattress, a poncho liner and a quiet place to lie down in the corner."

"That sounds okay. Now if you can point me to the sanitary facilities..."

Reese grinned. "That's even more primitive. All we have is a slit-trench latrine. But if you like, I'll go with you to make sure you don't fall in."

"How gallant."

"God knows I try."

After the trip to the slit trench, the air mattress and poncho liner bed proved to be reasonably comfortable, and Laura quickly fell asleep to the muted hiss of the squelch from the radio's loudspeakers.

THE CRASHING EXPLOSION of the first mortar round brought Laura out of a sound sleep. For a moment she was disoriented and didn't know where she was. The second explosion jarred her back to reality, and she sat up and looked around in terror. In the dim light from the battery lamp over the radios she saw Torres crouched at the base of the bunker wall, his arms over his head.

She scrambled out of bed and scurried across the floor on hands and knees to join him. Without hesitating, the radioman reached out and pulled her toward him, shielding her with his body. A third thunderous explosion sounded right outside the bunker. The shock rattled the radios and showered dust on them. Torres hugged her closer.

A fourth explosion was followed by cries of pain and shouts from the men on the perimeter. The radio burst into life, and Torres released Laura to grab the microphone. It was hard to follow the radio conversation, but it was obvious that some men had been hurt and Torres was calling for a Dust-off, a Medevac chopper—that much military slang she knew. As near as she could tell from the jargon and code words, four men had been hurt.

When no more explosions followed, Laura realized the attack was over. At the sound of the approaching chopper rotors she cautiously climbed to the top of the steps leading out of the bunker. A few yards away someone was holding a blue-white strobe to guide the Dust-off chopper in for a landing in the center of the camp. In the blinking light she saw running men carrying poncho-wrapped forms to the ship.

The men in the trenches were sending out a steady barrage of fire to cover the Dust-off while it was on the ground. Red tracers reached out from the perimeter and disappeared into the darkness. An occasional green tracer came back out from the jungle toward the camp, but each time the NVA fired, the red tracers sought out the enemy firing positions and converged on them.

With a flurry of dust blown up by the rotors, the Dust-off lifted into the air. As soon as it was clear, someone fired another small parachute flare, flooding the hilltop with a flickering yellowish light. She hadn't realized that night combat was so colorful. It would have been beautiful if she didn't know that the lights meant men were fighting and dying.

Finally everything was quiet again. Even the men quit shouting to one another in both English and Nung Chinese. Laura went back down the steps into the bunker, and Reese joined her a few minutes later. "You okay?" he asked.

"Yes, Torres made sure I was safe."

Without answering, Reese turned to the radioman. "Report Dust-off away and negative further at this time."

"Yes, sir."

"Make sure you stay put in here," Reese said, turning back to her. "We may get some more of this tonight." Before she could answer he was climbing the steps out of the bunker again.

After the night attack was over, Laura sat up for several hours with Torres trying to make sense of what was going on around her. Every few minutes the camp's 81 mm mortars would fire a couple of rounds out into the jungle to remind the NVA they weren't asleep. Each time the mortar tubes fired she flinched, and when the hollow crump of the rounds exploded a few seconds later, she flinched again.

Torres, however, seemed too busy on the radio even to notice. She wondered how he could be so calm. But as she well knew, a person could get used to anything, even explosions in the night.

Sometime in the early hours of the morning she went back to her makeshift bed and fell into a restless sleep. She awoke at dawn to the sound of low voices in the bunker. Reese was talking with a couple of his sergeants. When he saw that she was awake, he dismissed the men and gave her a steaming cup of coffee.

"I've got a chopper coming in at about nine," he said, "to take you back to Nha Trang."

"Thanks."

"Look—" he squatted beside her "—I'm really sorry about all of this and I'm not trying to give you the bum's rush. But, as you saw last night, this is a dangerous place for you right now."

"You've convinced me," she said, an edge of sarcasm in her voice. "I'll go home, be a good little girl and leave you to your war."

"I didn't mean it that way," he said quickly. "It's just that I can't give you a story here."

"I know. I'm sorry I put you out."

"You didn't. If I was back at Ban Phoc, I'd enjoy having you as a camp guest. But here I'm real busy right now." He checked his watch. "In fact, I have to get back to it. We have to rebuild the bunker that got hit."

"I'll be okay till the chopper comes."

"Good. I'll see you then."

Laura made her way to the slit-trench latrine Reese had shown her the previous night. Dropping her pants, she squatted over the trench and relieved her bladder. She wasn't embarrassed, but she was glad to see that the men respected her privacy and didn't look her way. It reminded her of what she had read about the communal baths in Japan where men and women bathed together. The nudity wasn't noticed.

She looked for toilet paper, and when she didn't see any, remembered the small roll from the C-ration pack that Reese had suggested she put in her pocket. It had seemed rather silly at the time, but now she realized why he had made a point of mentioning it.

Back at the bunker, Torres had another canteen cup of coffee going on his tin can stove and offered her a refill. She took it, and after repacking her bag, went outside to wait for her ride. The camp was a flurry of activity. Two small bulldozers were moving the red dirt around, and dozens of men shoveled it into sandbags while others stacked the filled bags. She looked around for Reese but didn't see him until she heard the rotors of the in-bound chopper.

As soon as the slick touched down, Reese appeared, grabbed her and her bag and almost ran to meet it. After helping her buckle herself in, he stepped back out onto the ground. "I'll call you the next time I get to Saigon!" he yelled over the whine of the turbine.

"Do that!" she yelled back as he turned away.

The pilot twisted the throttle and pulled pitch to the rotor blades. Its turbine whining, the Huey lifted off in a cloud of red dust and pivoted on its axis. The last thing she saw as the slick climbed for altitude was Reese walking down to the bunker that had been hit the night before. He didn't even look up when the chopper passed right over his head.

7

July 1, Dak Sang, RNV

With Laura winging her way back to Saigon, Reese could go back to fighting the war. One of the first things he did was to duck into the bunker and put a call through to the S-3, the operations officer, at CCC to request permission for limited offensive and recon operations in his AO. If he didn't get some of his people into the woods and find out what the NVA were doing out there, he deserved to get mortared every night.

To his dismay the CCC put him on hold, saying they would have to check higher before he could be given permission to protect himself. Reese immediately smelled a rat. In the case of Command and Control Central higher headquarters could only mean MACV-SOG Headquarters in Tan Son Nhut, and that meant talking to the SOG operations officer, Colonel Stewart A. Marshall. If Marshall was taking a personal interest in the operations of Dak Sang, they were all in deep kimchi.

While he waited for CCC to get back to him, Reese went down to the perimeter to see how the engineers' bunker-building work was progressing. If he couldn't send his people out to protect themselves, he'd better make sure they were ready to take another pounding during the night.

Captain Hemmings, the engineer officer, was with Sergeant Pierce, and the two men were inspecting the bunker that had taken a direct hit from an NVA 82 mm mortar round. Though one Nung had been killed and three wounded when the round detonated on top of the front wall, sending shrapnel through the open roof, it could have been worse. It could have hit squarely and killed them all.

"If you're going to get those kind of night visitors again," Hemmings said, "I'd better have my people concentrate on getting all the roofs built on these things before we finish putting up the walls."

"There'll be more of it," Reese said grimly. "I can almost guarantee you that."

"Can you give me some extra manpower to help with the roofing timbers and PSP?" Hemmings requested.

"Can do." Reese looked over at his team sergeant. "Sergeant Pierce will give you as many warm bodies as you need."

"Good," Hemmings said, turning to Pierce. "Just talk to Sergeant Gilmore. He'll tell you where he needs them."

"Will do, sir," Pierce said, just as he spotted the engineer sergeant a little farther down the perimeter.

As soon as Pierce reported that the Nung work parties had been given their assignments for the day, Reese took him off to one side. "We might have a little problem here. I think Marshall's got a stick in the fire for us."

"Now what?" Pierce asked. "Another suicide mission for the gallant Green Berets of A-410?"

"It's a suicide mission, all right, but we don't have to go anywhere to die this time. I've got a feeling he wants us to sit tight and let them come to us. I asked CCC if I could put some combat patrols out, and they told me they had to check with SOG first."

Pierce looked out over the valley. "If we don't start getting aggressive out there real soon, we're going to get our dicks knocked stiff."

"I know." Reese's voice was hard. "Regardless of what CCC says, we're going to have someone out in the woods tonight giving us a little early warning."

"I'll alert Kowalski and Hotchkiss," Pierce said. "We can send them out as listening posts with a Nung RTO, and nobody will be the wiser."

"I hate to expose them that way. But do it. Also, I want you to talk to Vao and Santelli about putting one of the platoons on a night-shift schedule."

"That's going to slow down the work on the camp if they're sleeping during the day," Pierce warned.

"I know," Reese said, "but we've got to have fresh, wide-awake bodies out there on the perimeter. I can't expect these men to build bunkers all day and then try to stay awake during the night."

"I'll get that set up right away, sir."

"Good. I'll be in the bunker if you need me."

DICK CLIFFORD MADE the long walk down the hall to Colonel Marshall's office with Reese's request in his hand. CCC's commander, Lieutenant Colonel Ronald had been given specific instructions to clear any

Dak Sang operation plans through SOG before granting their approval. Clifford was afraid this was just the first of what was going to be a long series of such walks. He still didn't know exactly what Marshall had in mind for Dak Sang, but whatever it was, he knew it was going to be bad news for Reese and the men of A-410.

Reese had pissed the colonel off, and as Clifford well knew, that wasn't a healthy thing to do.

After knocking on the door, Clifford halted the regulation three paces in front of the colonel's desk. "It's a message from A-410, sir," he said, handing the paper across the desk. "They got mortared again last night, one man KIA and three more wounded. Captain Reese is requesting permission to conduct combat patrols in the area around his camp to dislodge the mortar teams."

"They know he's there, do they?" Marshall smiled. "That's good, very good."

"Good, sir?"

"Yes," Marshall explained. "I want the NVA to know he's there. The Dak Sang camp is going to become a magnet, a dink magnet. Before too long every NVA unit passing through the area is going to try their hand at pushing Reese off his little hill."

"Isn't that similar to what the Marines tried to do at Khe Sanh?"

Marshall leaned back in his chair, a smug smile on his face. "Not really. The Khe Sanh operation was much too big to supply and support properly. There were so many troops there that they attracted the attention of several NVA divisions, and it required too much firepower to keep the situation under control. Here we'll only be dealing with battalions, an occasional regiment at the most. We'll be able to take them out easily. Tell Reese to go ahead and put his patrols out. Actually, that'll fit right in with the bigger picture. The more he beats around in the brush, the more he's going to attract attention, and that's exactly what I want him to do."

Clifford frowned. "But what's going to happen when he attracts a little more attention than he can handle with a single Mike Force Company and the artillery?"

Marshall leaned forward over his desk, a wolfish smile slowly forming on his face. "Then I've got a little surprise in store. Starting today, President Johnson's bombing restrictions are being canceled. We can go back to pounding them from the air. So, just as soon as Reese gets a bunch of them piled up in Cambodia, waiting to cross the border to hit him, I can send the Arc Light strikes in again."

Clifford hated to admit that the plan had some merit. The high-flying B-52 Arc Light bombing raids were one of the most effective tactics in use anywhere in Southeast Asia. In his opinion President Johnson had been a complete idiot to shut off the B-52 strikes in a vain attempt to save his presidency by coaxing the North Vietnamese to the conference table for peace talks.

After all this time he should have known that the only way to deal with the NVA was from a position of strength, not weakness. Halting the raids had been seen as a sign of weakness in Hanoi. The North Vietnamese had rewarded Johnson's naive plea for peace with increased military action in the South. As soon as the skies were clear of the deadly rain of bombs, they had upped the military traffic on the Ho Chi Minh Trail and had even attacked the capital again last month. Trying to deal with Hanoi from a standpoint of weakness was a fool's game, but that was typical of Johnson's entire conduct of the war.

"Tell Reese to protect himself," Marshall added. "I don't want them to get wiped out. I need them there."

"Yes, sir."

On his way to the radio room to send the message to Reese through CCC, Clifford wondered if he should try to fly out to Dak Sang and have a little confidential chat with the A-410 commander. Trying to contact him on the radio was out. Marshall went through the day's messages, but Reese needed to know what he was up against. Considering what they had been through last month, Clifford owed him that much.

It was a bone-weary Laura Winthrop who arrived back at her apartment in Cholon shortly after three. When the chopper dropped her off at the Army airfield in Nha Trang, she decided that rather than stay in town she'd go back to Saigon where she was determined to get to the bottom of the Dak Sang mystery. Reese might have his lips sealed, but she wasn't about to let that stop her. Like most of the press corps, she considered military security to be more of a challenge than a threat and wasn't put off by Reese's plea for caution.

After showering off the dust and dirt of her travels, she realized she still had time to make the daily press briefing at the MACV PIO office if she hurried.

Widely known as the "five o'clock follies," the briefing was MACV's opportunity to tell the press corps about any military activity that had taken place the previous day and night. The high command attempted to put their best foot forward, and the briefing was a real military "horse and pony show," complete with starched and spit-shined briefing officers, fancy charts, coffee, doughnuts and every amenity the taxpayers' money could buy. Instead of MACV putting their best foot forward, however, usually the foot ended up in their mouth, all the way to the knee.

A fast cab and an offer to pay twice the fare got her to the MACV building with five minutes to spare. Even though she didn't cover the actual combat part of the war, Laura had been to several of the briefings, and this one was typical. First off the official spokesman for the day, a young major with a football player's build, a movie star's toothy smile and a radio announcer's voice, reported that General Creighton Abrams had taken over command of MACV from General Westmoreland earlier that afternoon.

There was a thunderous round of applause after the brief announcement. The overly polished, politically correct Westmoreland hadn't been popular among the press corps. Right or wrong, most reporters felt that every time he had opened his mouth, he had been lying. They hoped that the blunt, plainspoken, cigar-chomping Abrams would be a little more up-front with them.

When the applause died down, the major went on to quickly recount the previous day's military operations. In the continued sweep of the area around Saigon another huge cache of rockets and weapons had been uncovered north of the city. The scheduled pullout of the Marines from Khe Sanh was progressing smoothly. No major contacts had been reported, but a Special Forces camp in the Delta had been attacked with twelve rounds of mortar fire, the Air Cav had lost a Huey to ground fire, and a line battalion of the Twenty-fifth Infantry Division had walked one of their companies into an ambush outside of Dau Tieng, losing four men.

On the noncombat side several more villages in the Delta were declared to be cleared of VC, the total tonnage of shipping into the outports had risen and the South Vietnamese draft had met its goals for the month.

At the end of his prepared spiel the major set aside his chrome-plated pointer and asked for questions from the audience. Laura shot her hand up, and the briefing officer immediately recognized her. The few women who attended the briefings usually asked easy questions, so he called on her first. "Yes, ma'am."

Laura stood to ask her question. "Why didn't you have a report on the shelling of the Special Forces camp at Dak Sang last night?"

The major frowned. "Dak Sang? I don't have a report on that incident."

"You had a report on that other Special Forces camp, the one in the Delta. Why not Dak Sang?"

"Sometimes we don't get the reports from Special Forces in time for the briefing," he said smoothly. "I'm sure I'll have something on that tomorrow, miss."

"Thank you," Laura said as she sat down.

The Major looked out over his audience. "Next."

Most of the reporters asked about the pullout from Khe Sanh and the new Marine firebase being established ten miles to the west, well outside the range of the NVA artillery in Cambodia. Some, however, raised questions about the progress of the peace talks in Paris.

The major responded to the questions about Khe Sanh, but declined to answer the inquiries concerning the Paris talks, saying that the press corps probably knew more about that than he did. After the Q and A session, Laura didn't stick around for coffee and doughnuts. She'd had enough MACV for one day. She had a definite feeling she'd been sandbagged on the Dak Sang issue. Her instincts told her there was more to the story than just a late combat report. Like any good reporter, she always followed her instincts.

On the way out she reached into her purse for her little black book of phone numbers. Surely she had to know someone who would be more than glad to talk in exchange for the pleasure of her company at dinner. After sorting through the MACV staff officer types she had met, she chose a likely candidate to grill. Borrowing the phone at the front desk, she placed a quick call.

8

July 1, Dak Sang

It was late afternoon by the time Reese received the go-ahead from CCC for a local recon of the area. Rogering the message, he quickly ordered Pierce to alert the Nungs for the upcoming patrol and to call the rest of the A-team together for a mission briefing.

The Special Forces men gathered quickly. They were tired of sitting around waiting to get shot at and were anxious to get back to doing what they did best—chasing down and killing the enemy before the enemy killed them. Also, they'd had more than enough of filling sandbags like grunts to last them for a long while.

"Okay," Reese said as soon as the six men were assembled in the bunker. "CCC has finally given us permission to move out into the woods and find out what in hell we're up against around here."

"It's about fucking time," Santelli muttered. Dodging mortar shells at night wasn't his idea of spending a restful evening. Additionally, as the team's executive officer, he was shouldering most of the burden of getting the new camp set up properly. A walk in the woods, even a combat patrol, would be a real rest for him.

"You've got that shit right, LT," Sergeant Gil Ko-walski said, voicing the feelings of the rest of the team. None of them were comfortable remaining in a purely defensive posture. The Special Forces philosophy of doing unto others before they did it to you meant taking the war to the enemy. Hiding in a hole while everyone in the world took potshots was for leg infantry units, not the Green Berets.

Reese turned to a large-scale map taped on the bunker wall. "I want three five-man recon patrols out there tonight," he said, tapping the map. "Jack, you'll take one team and will be the overall patrol leader. Ski, you and Larry will take the other two teams. Pack for three days, and by that time I should have the rest of guys up here and we'll relieve you."

Splitting the A-team to assist in turning over the old camp as well as trying to set up the new camp had stretched Reese's resources to the limit. With three men going out on patrol, Reese would have to run Dak Sang with just Pierce, Torres, Hotchkiss and Silk Wilson, the medic. Since the command bunker had to be manned twenty-four hours a day, Torres and Wilson would have to stand radio watch in the bunker twelve hours on and twelve off while Pierce, Hotchkiss and Reese supervised the engineers' construction work.

"Your primary mission out there," Reese continued, "will be to try to keep us from getting mortared again. Since the max range for the 82 mortar is some three thousand yards, I want you to stay within the three-klick mortar fan." He traced a circle on the map around the camp.

"Keep moving around out there and see what you can stir up. If you spot something, call it back and we'll put some artillery on it. You find something big, report it fast, then get the hell out and I'll see if I can call some air strikes in.

"The weather should be clear for the next few days with scattered cloud cover. Moonrise tonight is at 0320 and BMNT is 5:46."

BMNT, Beginning Morning Nautical Twilight, was that time of day, long before the sun came up, when it was possible to distinguish a target through a weapon's day sights at fifty yards. It also marked the time when a unit transitioned from night fighting techniques to daytime tactics.

"You boys are going to need to keep a real cool tool out there, though, and try to stay out of trouble. We've got the artillery laid on and maybe some Tac Air, but I don't have any lift ships standing by to pull your asses out if you step on your dicks. I want you to find 'em and to call in any targets you find, but stay out of firefights if you can avoid them. I don't have any way of reinforcing you or pulling you out quickly."

Reese looked at each of his men in turn. "You have any questions?"

"What happened to our Hatchet Force mission, sir?" Kowalski asked. "I thought we were going to do this Sneaky Pete, Hatchet Force shit across the fence, not sit on our asses and play pop-up targets for the enemy."

"So did I," Reese admitted. "But until we can get this camp built, we aren't going anywhere except our own local AO. And even then, if we can't get the local dinks to stop shooting at us, we still aren't going anywhere. We can hardly do a Sneaky Pete number with the dinks breathing down our necks day and night." He turned back to the map. "As soon as you can get out there and convince the bad guys to leave us alone, we can get on with the rest of the war."

"Okay," he said, glancing at his watch. "Night falls in about three hours and twenty minutes. More than likely we're under enemy observation, so don't be too obvious about getting ready. I'll see you all back here for a final briefing right after the sun goes down."

"Airborne!" Kowalski grinned, giving the traditional battle cry of the American parachute-trained troops, including the Special Forces.

"You'll think Airborne," Reese growled, "if you guys don't find those mortar teams. I need to get caught up on my beauty sleep."

"We'll find 'em for you, Captain," Kowalski promised with a grin. "You need all the help you can get."

SANTELLI WENT BACK to the unfinished sleeping bunker he would be sharing with Reese as soon as the camp was finished. He had been too busy even to start unpacking his gear, so he was already halfway prepared for the mission. All he had to do was sort through his gear, repack his rucksack, check his magazines, draw a couple of day's rations, and he would be ready to go.

As always, though, he broke down his weapons for a thorough cleaning. With the ongoing bulldozing and sandbagging, they were covered with a fine coating of red dust. As he well knew, a little moisture, even dew, would turn the powdery dust into sticky mud that could cause the weapon to jam at the worst possible time.

Cleaning his weapons was a form of meditation for the young officer, and he used it to put himself in the right frame of mind for the coming operation. It had been almost a month since he had been in the field, and he didn't want to screw something up because he wasn't mentally prepared to go to war.

Like all soldiers new to combat, Santelli had found himself wondering during his first few weeks in-country how he would react the first time he came under enemy fire. But when it finally happened, he'd been surprised to find he'd reacted exactly as he had been trained to do and that it had worked successfully just the way he had been told it would. When the brief firefight was over and he'd seen the bodies of the VC his ambush team had killed, he'd realized that leading men in combat was what he wanted to do more than anything else in the world.

From that time on he had gone out on missions every chance he could get, and he had developed into a savvy, well-experienced jungle fighter. If he had been asked what he was fighting for, Santelli couldn't have put it into precise words, certainly not the kind of words politicians used. Part of it, though, was his feeling that he was doing something worthwhile for his country, and part of it was his belief in people governing themselves. But had he been completely honest with himself, most of his reason for fighting was his addiction to the adrenaline surge of combat.

As the French Marshal Foch had said in World War I, "It is good that war is so terrible. Otherwise men would come to love it too much."

Santelli hadn't yet seen how terrible war could be, and he still loved it too much.

When he was satisfied that his weapons were ready, Santelli broke into a C-ration case to pick his meals. They were only scheduled to stay out for three days, but he packed coffee and TP for a couple of more days just in case. He could go without food if he had to, but he absolutely had to have his coffee and a proper wipe in the morning.

RIGHT AFTER DARK the Nungs and their Special Forces leaders assembled in the command bunker for a last-minute briefing.

The twelve Nung Strikers wore tiger stripe jungle fatigues and boonie hats, their faces and hands camouflaged with green and black grease paint. Most of them wore an Army-issue OD towel draped around the back of their necks as a sweat rag. On their backs they carried NVA-style rucksacks loaded down with a double basic load of ammunition and grenades as well as enough water and rations for three days. They would be humping almost sixty pounds a man, not counting their individual weapons, but they couldn't go out with any less.

Three of the young Nungs were further burdened with Prick-77 radios and extra batteries. The AN/PRC-77 radio had a secure voice capability that would prevent interception of their radio transmissions. Since the radios were their sole link to the camp, they didn't need anyone listening in on their conversations.

Most of the Nungs were armed with M-16s, but Santelli had taken the precaution of adding an M-60 machine gun to each one of the teams as well as a Thumper, an M-79 grenade launcher. Since the teams were so small and reinforcement was iffy, they might need the extra firepower if they made contact. The riflemen also carried extra bandoliers of 40 mm grenades for the Thumpers and extra link belts of 7.62 mm M-60 machine gun ammunition.

The three Special Forces men were also dressed in tiger suits and camouflage face paint, and they carried a mixed bag of weapons. Santelli had his Swedish K 9 mm submachine gun and his Browning 9 mm Hi-Power pistol. Tucked into his rucksack was the Ruger Mk.1 .22-caliber semiautomatic silenced pistol. The Ruger was insurance that he could make a silent kill if he needed to get out of a tough spot.

Gil Kowalski had his CAR-15, the shortened submachine gun version of the M-16 rifle, and carried an Army-issue .45-caliber pistol in a field belt holster as well as a Bowie knife taped upside down on his assault harness.

Larry Webb, the demo man, was equipped with an M-16 rifle as well as his favorite 12-gauge Remington automatic shotgun slung over his shoulder and a Browning Hi-Power 9 mm pistol in a shoulder holster. Firing double-ought buckshot, the shotgun was a good short-range weapon for this kind of work.

Reese had little to add to the afternoon's briefing, and CCC had no new information either about what they were facing. A last-minute check of weapons and equipment was made, watches were synchronized, the radios switched over to the proper frequencies, and the radio SOIs, the code books, hung around the team leaders' necks. They were ready.

"Good luck, Jack," Reese said to his lieutenant.

Santelli grinned. "You're the ones who need the luck, Captain. You're the scheduled target for the night, not us."

"I hope to hell not," Reese said. "That's why I'm sending you guys out there. I need a good night's sleep."

Santelli's answering laugh floated back behind him as he bounded up the stairs leading out of the bunker.

EARLIER THAT EVENING Santelli had gone to each of the fighting positions in the western sector of the perimeter to warn the Nungs about the outgoing patrol. This was no time to have somebody with a nervous trigger finger see movement in front of the wire and open up on them.

After meeting at one of the machine-gun bunkers, the patrol went out through the wire by teams, keeping low and making sure they stayed on the twisting, narrow path cleared through the mine fields. Once through the wire they formed up at the base of the hill and moved out into the jungle. If they ran into trouble now, they needed to be together so they could mass their firepower and make sure they didn't shoot each other up by mistake in the dark.

When the patrol was several hundred yards from the hill, Santelli called a halt. The Nungs formed a small defensive perimeter while the Americans huddled for a last-minute conference.

"This will be the assembly area if anything happens tonight," Santelli said. "If you get hit, try to make it back here and hold on until the captain can get reinforcements down to you. Any questions?"

There were none. Kowalski and Webb were old hands at this game. They knew full well that if they stumbled into the enemy that night, they'd never be able to make it back to the assembly area, much less the camp.

"Okay, then, let's go."

Santelli was the last to leave the patrol's assembly area. Taking up the point position, he led his team deeper into the jungle.

9

July 1, Saigon

It was only a few minutes before the ten o'clock curfew when Laura Winthrop let herself out of the yellow-and-blue Renault taxi at the French colonial-style villa on the edge of the Cholon district. The news service paid the rent for the big house and also provided the Vietnamese house staff to cook and clean and a small security force to guard the compound.

The old Nung on guard at the front gate raised his hand in a French-style salute when he recognized her.

"Ni hao, co ba," Laura said, using the Nung greeting Reese had taught her.

The guard grinned a gap-toothed smile as he opened the gate for her. *"Ni hao,* Missy Laura."

As she opened the front door, she saw that she wasn't the only one who was home early that night. The main room of the villa had been converted into a dayroom for the reporters. Several couches and overstuffed chairs were clustered around a big TV set and a pool table. The room was crowded with reporters who also had no place to go with the post-Tet Offensive citywide curfew in force. The curfew had been a great excuse to get away from her dinner date, but she had to admit that Saigon had been a lot more fun before the government-imposed curfew had closed down the late-night hot spots.

Her quest for information over dinner had been a bust. The only thing her date had wanted to do was get her drunk, for the obvious reasons. Every time she had tried to steer the conversation to Special Forces operations, the MACV staff major she had chosen from her list of possible informants as the one most likely to blab, had deftly changed the subject back to his favorite topic—himself.

After dinner he dropped some not-too-subtle hints about her going home with him, but she had insisted on staying at the bar until it was time to catch a cab home to beat the curfew. The MACV major had been thoroughly pissed, but then so was she. The evening had proved to be a complete waste of her time, and the food hadn't been that good, either. Now she was back to square one.

"Hey, Laura!" one of the reporters yelled from across the room where a card game was in progress. "Come over here and rub the back of my neck for good luck. I'm losing."

Rather than respond with some smart remark about where he could stick his hand, she decided to join in the game. She usually didn't play poker with the guys because they were poor losers and she had learned the game from a master of the pasteboards—her crazy Uncle Tom. But maybe she'd give them a lesson in cards. That is, if they had any tidbits about Special Forces operations they were willing to trade for a lesson in playing poker.

For the first few hands Laura made sure she lost, not too badly, nor too obviously, but she bet high and lost. The men, figuring they had a fish on the line, kept her glass full of gin and tonic as the cards were dealt. Not only had Laura learned how to play cards from her black sheep Uncle Tom, but also he had taught her to hold her liquor. All the guys were doing by trying to get her loosened up was getting themselves drunk instead.

After an hour and a half, Laura had the men right where she wanted them—drunk and talkative. She started winning consistently, and after scooping up a large pot, paused for a break as she shuffled the cards. "Maybe you guys can help me. I'm trying to do a story on the Special Forces, and I'm having a lot of trouble with it."

"Screw those super soldiers," one reporter said. "You ought to be doing a story on us instead. You know, the brave combat correspondents risking their lives to bring the truth to the American people. And—" he thumped himself on the chest "—you could start by interviewing me as a sterling example of the breed."

Laura looked over her cards. "And I suppose you want me to do the interview in your room later tonight, right?"

That brought a big chuckle from the other men.

"Of course," the reporter said. "I'm always at my best in my own room."

"Somehow I doubt that," Laura said dryly. "But I'm willing to listen to anything you can tell me about the SF operations along the border."

"What side of the border are you talking about?" one of the older men spoke up.

Laura took a gamble. "The other side."

The man sat back and took a long pull at his beer. "That's an interesting story idea. But you can't quote me on anything I tell you."

Laura put on a look of complete innocence. "I'd never do that without asking you first."

"Well," he said, "most of what I've heard is rumor, but there's definitely something going on over there. Something they're hiding from us."

Laura didn't have to ask who the "they" were that he claimed was hiding information from the press. In this case it could only be the Army brass at MACV.

"What have you heard?" she protested.

"Well, it seems like there's a whole other war going on outside Vietnam."

"Who's running it?"

The man smiled. "That's the real question."

Intrigued by his answer, Laura leaned across the table. "Who do you think's running it, then?"

The man's smile widened.

THE MOON WASN'T UP YET, so Santelli's movement through the pitch-black jungle was slow. The foliage wasn't as thick in the valley around Dak Sang as it was in some of the other places in Southeast Asia, but it was still rugged going. Every few hundred yards or so he halted his team and listened for any sounds of the enemy. So far the only things he'd heard were the normal sounds of night life in the jungle.

Usually that would be a good sign, but since they were hunting the enemy, it wasn't good. Had the jungle been unnaturally quiet that would have meant the NVA were also moving through the jungle. For this operation to pay off he had to find the enemy.

Moving out again, Santelli changed his route and headed in a more northerly direction. Wherever the enemy was tonight he was determined to find them.

At the next halt Santelli noticed that it had become quieter. The nocturnal inhabitants of the jungle weren't sounding their mating calls, and there were fewer hunting cries of the predators and death screams of their prey. In the jungle the lesser predators remained silent when the major predators roamed, predators armed with weapons more efficient than mere teeth and claws.

Rather than rest in place, Santelli became a predator himself, slipping through the brush with the silence of a hunting tiger. The NVA were near; he could almost smell them. The Nungs followed their team leader, their ears acutely tuned to pick up even the slightest noise, their eyes straining to see a flash of movement or the shadowed outline of the enemy.

The jungle was almost completely silent, and Santelli dropped behind a large tree. He signaled to the Nungs to cover him while he went forward. The one called "Cowboy," the team's interpreter, broke away and silently followed the lieutenant.

A few yards farther on Santelli went to ground again, his thumb resting on the safety of the Swedish K. He started when Cowboy slipped up beside him but recovered and lightly touched the Nung's mouth and ear, telling the man to be silent and listen. At night the ears could be as effective as the eyes as long as you knew what to listen for.

A faint metallic clink sounded from about fifty yards in front of them. Santelli tapped the Nung on the shoulder, and the two men cautiously moved forward. Now they heard low voices speaking Vietnamese, the occasional click of metal on metal and the sound of rustling cloth. They had finally found their NVA mortar crew.

"Trung Si," the Nung interpreter whispered urgently in Santelli's ear, "they Cong, and they say they going to shoot at the camp tee tee."

That sounded reasonable, and Santelli knew he had to get some artillery on them before the first round could be dropped down the mortar tube. Since he didn't know their numbers it would be foolish to try to take them out with just the small arms of his team. Besides, Reese had wisely told him to stay out of firefights. Santelli and the Nung backed away from their observation point with great stealth. Listening for the enemy at night could work both ways.

When he got back to the rest of his team, Santelli took out his poncho liner, made a tent over himself and studied his map in the light of his red-filtered flashlight. As soon as he had plotted the NVA's location on the map, he whispered to the Nung RTO for the radio handset.

Keying the mike, he spoke softly. "Bent Talon, Bent Talon, this is Talon Five. Fire mission, over."

"This is Bent Talon," Torres's voice replied, sounding loud over the handset. "Send it."

"This is Five. I've spotted what I think is a mortar team, and we need a little HE on them. Grid 873527. Azimuth 273, range six hundred. Will adjust, over."

"Bent Talon, roger. Wait out."

A few moments later a new voice came in over the radio. It was from the Artillery FDC, the fire direction center, of the battery at Firebase Rhonda that was tasked with supporting the camp. "Belt Talon Five, this is Red Leg Five Niner. Shot over."

"Talon Five, shot out," Santelli said, acknowledging that he understood the first round had been fired.

The firebase was too far away to hear the firing of the big guns, but he heard the express-train rushing of a 155 mm howitzer round flying through the air. A second later the jungle was lit up with the flash of the detonation of the ninety-five-pound high-explosive shell. The round had hit beyond and a little to the left of his target.

"This is Red Leg Five Niner. Splash over."

"Talon Five, splash," Santelli said, acknowledging that he had seen the strike of the first round. "Right five zero, drop one hundred. Battery two, fire for effect, over."

"This is Five Niner," the Artillery FDC answered. "Copy right five zero, drop one hundred, battery two, fire for effect, over."

"Talon Five, roger good copy."

"This is Five Niner. Wait out."

There was a short pause while the guns were loaded and the corrections calculated. "Five Niner, shot over."

"Talon Five, shot out."

What had been the sound of a single train before became the roar of a hundred locomotives as six 155 mm rounds cut through the air simultaneously. The jungle suddenly erupted as over five hundred pounds of HE sent red-hot, razor-sharp shards of machined steel lancing through the jungle, shredding flesh and foliage alike. Another eruption followed a few seconds later when the artillery battery fired again.

As the echoes of the last detonation faded away, the jungle was completely silent and, in the sudden stillness, Santelli heard moans of pain and shouts as the survivors tried to help their wounded comrades. This was a good time for the team to get the hell out of there before anyone got the bright idea to go looking for them.

They all scrambled to their feet, and Santelli led his team away as fast as he could. Five hundred yards farther on they stopped again for a brief rest and to get their bearings. Under the cover of his poncho again he checked the map and took a compass bearing for another area he wanted to patrol. The artillery attack would have made the NVA move out of the area, but maybe they'd get lucky somewhere else.

After a fifteen-minute break, the team took off again, angling away to the west, closer to the border. They continued on through the night, halting only every half hour or so to listen. When the moon came up, the team spent more time sitting and watching, but they made no more contact. It appeared that the NVA had gone to ground after the artillery attack.

THE FIRST TENDRILS of dawn were streaking the hill-tops on the west side of the valley when a weary Santelli and his team halted in a small clump of brush on a low rise. There was no high ground in the valley that would give them good observation of the terrain below, so this was the best location he could find.

They would spend the day there, sleeping in turns, watching the surrounding area and waiting for night to fall again. It was boring, but at least they wouldn't be back at Dak Sang filling endless sandbags and building bunkers.

After reporting his location to Reese, Santelli grabbed a quick C-ration breakfast of pound cake and fruit cocktail. Stuffing the empty cans back into his ruck, he found a soft spot on the ground and wrapped himself up in his warm poncho liner to get a little sleep before his turn came around to stand guard.

10

July 2, MACV-SOG Headquarters

The first thing Dick Clifford did after downing a quick cup of coffee was to take Reese's after-action report down the hall to Colonel Marshall. He should have taken the report to the colonel before he had his coffee, but he wasn't quite up to facing his boss without his morning caffeine fix.

A smile slowly formed on Marshall's face as he read over the report of the previous night's action in the woods around Dak Sang. A-410 was starting to attract quite a bit of enemy attention, and that meant his plan was working. He only had to up the ante, and he was sure the NVA would respond in kind.

"This is great," Marshall said. "Just great."

Clifford didn't bother to reply to Marshall's comment, but he was certain Reese didn't think it was "great" to have the woods around his new camp crawling with the enemy, who shot at him every night.

The colonel put the report in his in box and leaned back in his leather chair. "Get on the horn to Reese and tell him I want more of his people out in the woods ASAP. I want them out there kicking ass and taking names. None of this Mickey Mouse Special Forces sneak-through-the-woods crap. He's starting to get results, and I want him to keep it up."

"Yes, sir."

"And," Marshall continued, "make sure CCC's got the artillery and air support I requested laid on for him. When he calls for help, I want it to be there waiting for him."

"Yes, sir."

LAURA WOKE LATER that morning bright and cheerful. She didn't even mind the fifty dollars she had allowed herself to lose as a sop to the male egos of the card players last night. As far as she was concerned, it had been money well spent. It had bought something she could finally use. It wasn't much, but she felt it was the genuine article and proved that she was on the right track.

She reached into her pocket and pulled out a faded, sweat-stained pocket patch one of the men had given her last night. The insignia showed a skull wearing a green beret set against a red jagged background almost like a stylized bomb burst. The letters *SOG* were stitched in black on a yellow scroll below the skull. The reporter had obtained the patch during the Tet Offensive when he found it sewn inside the green beret of an American Special Forces casualty.

The patch wasn't much to go on, but it went a long way to prove the existence of an organization that was supposedly running a secret war outside Vietnam. And it was an organization no one seemed to know anything about. MACV published a handy reference chart of the various military insignia worn in Vietnam, and it took no more than a brief glance to confirm that the patch wasn't on the official chart.

The other military insignia depicted swords, eagles, wings and various stylized, colorful designs that had nothing to do with the grim reality of the war—death. The SOG patch, however, was right up-front about it. Whatever SOG was, it had to do with death, and specifically death in the form of the Special Forces.

A couple of quick phone calls to a source at MACV answered many of her questions. For one, she learned that the intials SOG were properly pronounced as a word, *Sog,* as in soggy. Secondly she learned that the initials stood for Studies and Observations Group, some kind of military think tank that studied the weather in Southeast Asia and its effects on combat operations in the region.

It was a good lead, but it seemed strange that an organization supposedly studying the weather should have an insignia depicting death personified in the guise of the U.S. Special Forces. She didn't need to be Sherlock Holmes to know that someone was pulling her chain in a big way.

SOG obviously existed—she had the patch and she had a fanciful cover story about them—but somehow she didn't think the organization had anything to do with passive studying and observing, unless they were studying better ways to kill people and were observing the results. The iconography of their insignia suggested that was precisely what they were doing.

There were still a couple of puzzling questions left. What was a man like Mike Reese doing working for a secret organization of elite Green Beret killers, and what was going on at Dak Sang? One way or the other she was determined to find out.

The problem was that she had very little to go on except for the cover story and the name Reese had inadvertently dropped. She had no first name or rank to go with it. But judging by Reese's concern, it was a fair bet that Marshall had to be a senior officer, probably a colonel or general.

Suddenly she recalled something Reese had mentioned on the night they had had dinner in Saigon. The increased NVA traffic on the Ho Chi Minh Trail had been the topic of discussion, and he had mentioned the Studies and Observation Group. He had also supplied her with a name if she wanted information.

Now what in hell had that name been? She vaguely remembered jotting something down in her small notebook that night. Digging it out of her purse, she looked in the back where she kept her notes, and there it was: Dick Clifford, Studies and Observations Group, Tan Son Nhut. There was no phone number, but that shouldn't be hard to find.

On second thought she decided that giving Clifford a phone call wasn't necessarily a good idea. If she called, he could easily hang up on her. Also, calling him could tip him off that she was on to their little game. It would be better to visit in person and try to talk to him, a journalistic ambush, as it were. As she well knew, it was always harder to put someone off face-to-face.

After a quick breakfast, Laura went through her wardrobe, searching for exactly the right thing to wear. She wanted to look professional, a real Lois Lane, but at the same time she knew she had to look sexy. Not too sexy, though, or she ran the risk of being dismissed as a bimbo. She had to look tough, professional and sexy.

Finally she selected an outfit and took a quick shower. Once she was dressed she hurried downstairs to hail a cab for the long ride to the Air Force base at Tan Son Nhut.

WHEN REESE AND PIERCE inspected the camp that morning, they saw that Captain Hemmings's engineer troops had really busted their asses the day before. Evidently the mortar attack had acted as an added incentive to get the work done. With the bulldozers to move the red dirt and the Nungs filling sandbags, the work on the camp was progressing well. A couple of more days like yesterday and they would be ready for anything.

Unlike many of the Mike Force border camps, Dak Sang was not star-shaped or pentagonal; it was circular. For one thing, the natural shape of the hill lent itself to a circular-shaped perimeter. Also, with their limited numbers, the circular perimeter presented the smallest possible length of wire to defend and still contain the living area the men of A-410 needed.

The outer perimeter was comprised of three rings of wire obstacles, both concertina and razor wire, strung on steel posts driven into the ground. The rings were spaced five yards apart, and the area between them was laced with tanglefoot, a spiderweb of barbed wire set at twelve- and eighteen-inch intervals above the ground.

Placed in both the concertina and the tanglefoot were hundreds of trip flares, small pressure-sensitive mines and command-detonated claymore antipersonnel mines. Reese had been glad to see the shithookload of flares and claymores show up on the second day. For the past several months claymores had been in short supply, and only now was production catching up with the post-Tet demand for them.

The M-18A1 claymore mine had been designed for use against mass assaults and was one of the most effective weapons for camp defense. The mine was a curved rectangular plastic casing containing a little over a pound of C-4 plastic explosive and several hundred .25-caliber steel balls. When the antipersonnel mine detonated, the steel balls flew out in a sixty-degree, fan-shaped pattern and were lethal to a range of fifty yards.

Some of the electrically fired claymores were set up as booby traps and others were controlled by the troops in the bunkers. Yet another set was controlled by a master switch in the command bunker to be used as a last-ditch defense if the enemy stormed the wire.

The fighting bunkers were all started. Sergeant Pierce and Santelli had sited them in carefully so that there were no dead spots in their overlapping defensive fire. The twelve machine-gun bunkers were close enough that they could cover each other during an assault. Supplemental fighting trenches had been dug between the bunkers, and the forward side of the trench was well sandbagged with individual fighting positions.

The next step would be to mix cement with the red dirt to make a rust-colored concrete that would be plastered over the exposed sandbags to keep the torrential monsoon rains from reducing the fortifications to a bog. But for now the sandbags were bare.

The command bunker had received its roof, and the last of the sandbags were being placed on top. While right behind it the sandbagged electric generator had been put in place and the electric lights were being installed. By nightfall they could plug in the radios and minirefrigerators and still have enough power to show movies to the strikers on the nights they were in camp. The Nungs loved to watch movies, particularly World War II ones. To them the Germans and Japanese were the VC.

The sight that brought Reese the most pleasure, however, were the heavy weapons emplacements that were now under construction. The two M-40A1 106 mm recoilless rifles and the three M-29 81 mm mortars had finally been brought up from their old camp at Ban Phoc late yesterday. At last they had some heavy firepower they controlled on their own instead of relying on artillery support that might or might not be available when most needed. Reese always felt uneasy when he didn't have something on hand with a little punch to it.

The mess hall was almost finished, and the engineers were laying out the floors for the dispensary, the showers and the sleeping quarters. The last thing to be built was the strikers' canteen and tea shop. When it was completed, Dak Sang would truly be the new home for Reese's Nungs.

In just a few more days Dak Sang would be completely ready for business. As soon as the construction work was finished, Reese could finally put A-410 on a fully operational basis. After all, Marshall had sent them up there to be a Hatchet Force, not a Dak Sang Camp defense force.

WHEN REESE WENT BACK to the command bunker, he met Torres coming up the steps with a message form in his hands. "We got us a hot one, Captain," the radioman called out when he saw his commander.

Reese quickly read the message. CCC's orders were to take offensive action in their AO immediately. Their mission was to track down and destroy the NVA elements who had been sniping at them at night. Reese grinned as he handed the message back to Torres. It was high time they got their asses back out in the woods where they belonged.

"Call Santelli and his people back here ASAP," he said. "It's a whole new ball game now, and we've got to get ready for it."

"Yes, sir."

While Torres left to call in the patrols, Reese hurried to find Pierce. He wanted the Nungs alerted and ready so that when Santelli and the two sergeants returned, they could pick up their new units and go right back out into the jungle again. This time, however, they would be going with enough troops to fight instead of just creeping around in the bush.

11

July 2, MACV-SOG Headquarters

Laura's press card got her through the main gate at Tan Son Nhut, and a young AP on guard was glad to tell her how to get to the SOG building. In fact, he hadn't been able to take his eyes off her throughout his drawn-out directions when she could clearly see the building from the gate.

The two MPs at the SOG building's entrance, however, were another matter entirely. They were impressed with her bustline, too, but not enough to let her stroll inside. She wasn't on the list of authorized visitors, they informed her, and that was that. She wasn't getting into the building as long as they were guarding it.

"How do I get my name on the list?" she asked.

The MP shrugged. "Beats the hell outta me, lady. All I do is check the names, not put 'em on the list."

"Look, Sergeant," she said, "I need to talk to Dick Clifford in the Studies and Observations Group."

The MP's eyes narrowed when he heard the SOG cover name, but he didn't budge. "Sorry 'bout that, miss. I have my orders."

"I'd like to speak to your officer, then," Laura said, putting a touch of ice into her voice.

The MP shrugged and picked up the phone. The Army didn't pay him to argue with reporters, even good-looking blond female reporters. Maybe the LT could get it through this woman's thick head that she wasn't on the access list.

The MP officer turned out to be a baby-faced second lieutenant in his early twenties who was trying very hard to appear grown-up. Laura immediately pegged him for a rookie. "You wanted to see me, ma'am?"

Laura was only a few years older than the lieutenant, but his use of the honorific made her feel like his mother, and that annoyed her considerably. "Lieutenant Dillard, is it?" she said, reading his name tag.

He stood a little straighter. "Yes, ma'am. How can I help you?"

"Well, Lieutenant, I'm Laura Winthrop of UPI, and I want to speak to a Mr. Dick Clifford of the Studies and Observations Group."

Mentioning her press agency in the same sentence with SOG's cover name got the desired results. Dillard froze for a moment. "Ah...ah..."

"Why don't you call him," Laura prompted, "and let me talk to him?"

"I'll see if he's in, ma'am," Dillard said, anxious to pass the buck. He had only been on the job two weeks and was scared of screwing up. When Dillard returned, he looked relieved. "He'll be right down, ma'am."

Clifford turned out to be a tall, thin, cadaverous man wearing a bright Hawaiian shirt, tan slacks and aviator's sunglasses. Because of the sunglasses she couldn't read his eyes, but his posture indicated that he was very displeased. "I understand you want to see me, miss?"

Laura stuck out her hand and introduced herself. Clifford shook her hand, but then dropped it as if it were on fire when she announced her press affiliations.

"Where did you get my name?" he asked, when what he really wanted to know was how she had gotten a line on the Studies and Observations Group.

She smiled sweetly. "The press has its informants, too. And I'm sure you'll understand when I say that I can't reveal my sources."

Clifford understood what she was saying only too well. "What do you want?" he almost snapped.

"I'd like to have an interview with General Marshall."

"That's Colonel Marshall," Clifford automatically corrected. "And that just isn't possible, miss."

Bingo. Laura smiled to herself. Now she knew who this mysterious Marshall guy was. "Why can't I talk to him?"

"He doesn't give interviews," Clifford explained. "He doesn't like reading his name in the paper."

That was exactly the wrong thing to say to a reporter, and Laura went in for the kill. "If I don't get to talk to him," she said sweetly, "I can guarantee you that he'll see his name in print before the week's out."

Now Clifford was caught between a rock and a hard place. Marshall would have his guts for garters if this reporter stood good on her threat. But he also knew that if he called the colonel about an interview, he was putting his neck as well as his career on the line. Damn it, anyway, why did things like this always happen to him?

"Wait here, please."

LAURA WAS IMPRESSED with the dark wood-paneled walls, the Oriental rugs, the huge oak desk, leather furniture and the mahogany sideboard and bar when she was ushered into Marshall's office. She hadn't been in a senior officer's office before and didn't know that the opulence was standard Army-issue for bird colonels and generals stationed in Saigon.

The colonel, though, wasn't as impressive as his surroundings. Marshall looked like any of a hundred other senior officers she had seen at MACV. He was of average height and weight with a slight middle-age bulge around his waist and a touch of gray at the temples. Had his hair been a little longer he would have looked like any mid-level businessman worried about his sales figures, not the head of a secret organization.

When she introduced herself, he took her offered hand as though he were holding a poisonous snake. "Have a seat, please."

When she sat down in the plush red leather chair in front of Marshall's desk, she noticed that the colonel's eyes didn't automatically follow the movement of her bare, tanned legs when she crossed them. This was one man who couldn't be softened up with a little flash of skin. He was committed to his work.

Marshall ordered coffee, but Laura refused his hospitality. She wanted to get right to the interview.

"What can you tell me about your Studies and Observations Group, Colonel?"

"There's really not much to tell," he replied smoothly. "We make weather observations throughout Southeast Asia and study their impact on combat operations."

"You're using Green Berets as weathermen?" Laura asked, the tone of her voice not hiding her skepticism.

"Actually," Marshall said, "most of our personnel are civilians, people transferred from the U.S. Weather Service, that sort of thing. We only use the Special Forces personnel for observations along the border regions."

Obviously this was a carefully prepared cover story, and Laura knew a sandbag job when she saw one. She played her trump card. Reaching into her purse, she pulled out the battered SOG patch and placed it on the desk in front of the colonel. "And do all your weathermen wear this?"

When Marshall glanced down at the grinning skull with the green beret, his face hardened. The SOG patch was completely unauthorized, and wearing it was strictly forbidden. But fighting men like to die under their own colors, and almost every man in the SOG program had one of the patches. The forbidden insignia was also found on coffee mugs, Zippos, letterheads and any other place a SOG trooper could think to put it.

"Where did you get this?" he growled.

"I got it from one of my sources."

Marshall was smart enough not to ask about the source. "And just exactly what do you think it represents?"

"I think it's the key to the secret about SOG."

"Just what do you think this secret is?"

"SOG doesn't study the weather. SOG kills people."

"There is a war on, you know."

"Don't fuck with me, Colonel," Laura snapped.

Marshall's face went white. No one talked to him that way, least of all some bimbo reporter. "I think this interview is at an end, Miss Winthrop," he said, his hand reaching for the intercom buzzer on his desk.

Laura slowly got to her feet. "Twenty-four hours after I walk out of here, Colonel," she said, "your organization is going to be on the front page of every newspaper in the nation and by the six o'clock news of all three television networks. By the next day SOG will be a household word."

Marshall's hand slowly pulled away from the button. "Just exactly what is it you're after, miss?" His voice was clipped and he bit off each word.

Laura sank back down into the chair. "I want to do a story on SOG and the men in it, specifically a story on the Mike Force at A-410."

After she said that, Laura felt that if looks could kill, she would have died a messy death right in that office. She also had a feeling that Mike's body would be sprawled on the floor right next to hers.

"Did you get that patch from Captain Reese?" Marshall ground out.

"No, sir," Laura hastened to say. "In fact, Captain Reese has done everything in his power to keep me from learning about what he does for a living."

Marshall was silent for a moment.

"I met Mike Reese a month ago," she explained. "And I can say that he's a better liar than you are. He didn't disclose anything about his job except that he was in a Green Beret Mike Force Unit. When I learned about SOG later—on my own, I might add—I wanted to talk to him about it since he was the only Green Beret I knew. When I couldn't find him at his old camp, I tracked him to a remote place on the border called Dak Sang. I flew up there—"

Laura paused for a moment when she noticed that Marshall was visibly startled, but then she plunged on. "But he put me on a plane back to Nha Trang without saying a word." She leaned forward in her chair. "Now I want to know what in hell's going on. I want to do a story on SOG, and I think the American people have a right to know."

"You want to know 'what's going on,'" Marshall parroted, slowly shaking his head. "Woman, you don't have even the slightest idea what you're getting yourself into."

Laura was taken aback by his use of the word *woman* in that tone of voice. Coming from his lips, it sounded like a curse. "I'm also a reporter," she snapped back.

Marshall was silent for a moment. "I think the thing that you people forget," he said, "is that the so-called press corps in Vietnam is actually nothing more than a worldwide intelligence-gathering service for the North Vietnamese government.''

Laura frowned. "I don't understand what you mean, Colonel."

"It's very simple, miss. You people scream about your 'right' to print every damn thing you see or hear. You don't care in the least if your 'hot' story causes the unnecessary loss of American lives or gives valuable information about our operations to the enemy. You'll print it, anyway. The North Vietnamese are the biggest Asian subscribers to the major American newspapers and magazines. Every last thing you write they read."

"But there's the freedom of the press to consider."

"Bullshit," Marshall snorted. "If you'll pardon my French, Miss Winthrop. The First Amendment of the Constitution was never intended to allow reporters to release information vital to the nation's defense, or information that would cause American casualties during a war. In previous wars the press acted in a responsible manner. They either censored themselves or allowed themselves to be censored for the good of the war effort. In this war, however, every hack writer who can afford a plane ticket to Saigon sees himself as a future media superstar. The first thing they do when they hit town is to start planning their acceptance speeches at next year's Pulitzer Prize dinner."

"Don't you think that's a bit cynical, Colonel?"

"No, miss—" he shook his head "—I don't. All you have to do to see my point is to look at the hysteria the media generated about the Tet Offensive. Tet was a stunning military victory, but it was turned into a defeat by the press.''

He leaned forward over his desk. ''Or, for another example, look at this story you want to do on A-410. You're more than willing, anxious even, to expose one of the war's most successful long-term operations for your own personal aggrandizement.''

''That's not fair, Colonel.''

''Isn't it?'' He raised an eyebrow. ''You come storming in here and threaten me with blackmail if I don't go along with your little scheme. And, as far as I can tell, you really don't give a damn about who will be hurt. You're a reporter and you have your sacred 'rights.' Well, how about the rights of those men who will have their asses hanging in the wind as a result of this story you want to do. What about their rights?''

Laura was thoughtful for a moment. ''What if I agree to submit the story to you for censorship?''

''What kind of censorship?''

''Let's say that I agree to let you review the story to make sure I haven't revealed any secret classified information?''

''Miss Winthrop,'' Marshall said patiently, ''even the existence of this organization is highly classified. Exactly how high, I can't tell you, either. In fact, there's nothing you could write about SOG that I could let you print. Nothing at all.''

''What if I only write about the Mike Force?'' she asked. ''And don't mention SOG.''

Marshall thought for a moment. He knew Laura had him by the short hairs, and he had to do something before she blew SOG's cover and jeopardized the entire operation. "That might be possible, if I can censor the story and if I can have your word as a loyal American that you won't reveal anything about the Studies and Observations Group without my say-so."

"It's a deal, Colonel."

12

July 2, Dak Sang

This was a very different mission preparation than the one Reese had conducted for his antimortar patrols. Now that Marshall had finally turned him loose to take the war to the enemy, the full resources of SOG would be available for him to draw on. Specifically he could call on their supporting firepower and their up-to-date field intelligence on the enemy activities in their AO.

For the first time since they had arrived at Dak Sang, Reese would be completely plugged into the operations center of his Command and Control unit instead of taking his orders directly from the SOG headquarters in Tan Son Nhut. In fact, Reese had been so busy with the new camp that he hadn't even made the mandatory courtesy call on his new commander at CCC, Lieutenant Colonel Newman. This would be a good time to get that overdue chore out of the way and check in with CCC's S-3 section at the same time.

Torres was able to get a courier flight to Kontoum, and an hour later Reese was on his way. Command and Control Central had their own small compound a half mile south of the main American installation on the main road running south to Pleiku. It wasn't much as far as American camps went, but it wasn't surrounded with the usual bars, laundry and cathouses that had sprung up around other U.S. installations no matter how small. SOG had a way of keeping their distance even from the most persistent Vietnamese entrepreneurs. When CCC's Green Berets wanted to get steamed and creamed, they had to walk the half mile to town to do it.

The headquarters building was typical of a small compound: a single-story wooden structure with sandbags stacked halfway up the sides of the walls and a layer covering the sheet metal roof. The interior was also typical of a small unit headquarters. Plaques, photos and military memorabilia covered the bare plywood walls. The furniture was all well-worn GI issue even down to the battered mess-hall coffee maker on top of the steel filing cabinet. The CCC building was a stark contrast to SOG's plush quarters, but a combat headquarters was always sparse. Reese immediately felt right at home as he was ushered into the commander's office.

Lieutenant Colonel Ronald Newman was a thin, wiry man with short-cropped dark blond hair and vivid blue eyes. He was young for his rank, but he bore his silver oak leaves with confidence. On first impression Reese felt that he was going to like working for the man.

"I'm sure as hell glad to finally have you cleared for operations, Reese," Newman said after Reese had introduced himself and had been offered a seat. The colonel hesitated for a moment. "I don't exactly know what kind of deal you have with Colonel Marshall," he finally said. "First he wanted you held back for some reason, but this order to send you out immediately into the woods comes at exactly the right time. I need another SLAM company for an operation we have going."

"SLAM, sir?"

"Search, Locate, Annihilate Mission units," Newman explained. "They're ready-reaction forces we can use to exploit an RT sighting. We're assigned SLAM companies, but we also use the Hatchet Force units for backup SLAM missions when everyone else is busy."

"Sounds good to me, sir."

Newman walked over to a large map on the wall. "I've had RT Ghost tracking an NVA company for the past three days." He pointed to an area right inside the Cambodian border. "And it looks like the dinks are moving directly down into your AO. I want to sic you on those guys so I can pull that RT the hell out of there before they get spotted."

"We're ready to do it, sir," Reese said. "I'd much rather get a whack at 'em before they get close enough to mortar us again."

"I thought you'd feel that way, and my S-3 has been busy putting together a two-platoon operation for you."

Reese smiled. "I'm ready to talk to him about it, sir."

The major who ran the S-3, the operations staff, for CCC was an older man, tall and thin with close-cropped light blond, almost white hair and pale blue eyes. He looked like an older, more washed-out version of his commander and carried himself with just a hint of aristocratic bearing.

"I'm Jan Snow," he said, introducing himself with a faint European accent as he took Reese's hand. He pronounced the *J* in his name as a *Y.*

The Green Beret officer, once a refugee from the Hungarian Revolution in 1956, planned and ran the RT, Hatchet Force and SLAM operations for CCC and was known as the master of the cross-border operations. Snow viewed his job of ridding Southeast Asia of Communists as only a convenient way to pass the time until he could return to his homeland and drive out the Communists who kept his country enslaved.

Snow's hatred for the followers of Marx and Lenin ran deep. In the street fighting during the revolution a 122 mm cannon shell from a Russian JS III tank had destroyed a second-story street-front flat in a Budapest apartment building. Snow's young wife of two years and their baby daughter had been in the flat when the shell hit.

When the American assistance that President Eisenhower had promised failed to appear, the Hungarian Revolution collapsed under the weight of Russian armor, and Snow escaped to Austria. From there he made his way to the United States where he immediately enlisted in the Army. He took the name Snow as a nom de guerre upon his enlistment because his Hungarian name was too difficult for most Americans to pronounce.

Like many of his fellow countrymen, Snow was soon recruited into the newly formed Army Special Forces and, after further training, was commissioned as an officer. He had been in and out of Southeast

Asia since the earliest days of the American involvement, and all of his in-country work had been in covert operations.

The name on his paycheck stub read Snow, but the men he worked with called him the "Ice Man," and with good reason. When he planned and executed an operation, he was as cold and as hard as ice. Like everyone else in Special Forces, Reese had heard of the Ice Man's exploits and felt honored to have a chance to work with him.

Snow got right down to business and walked over to the large-scale map on the wall. "RT Ghost has been tracking a North Vietnamese company for the past four days now." His fingers traced a route on the map. "As you can see, projecting their track puts them right in your AO in another day or two. They're still in Cambodia now, and our best chance to stop them cold is to hit them before they cross over the border. Here's what I want you to do," the S-3 said, pulling down a clear acetate overlay. "One of your platoons will move out tomorrow morning at 0700. An hour later..."

THE MINUTE THE HUEY touched down outside the wire, Reese hit the ground running. As soon as he found Pierce, he sent him to bring the team ASAP for a mission briefing. When the men quickly assembled in the bunker, Reese was pleased to see that the rest of his A-team had finally joined up with them. He was going to need the full team to man the coming operation and still have someone to leave behind to defend the camp.

"Okay, people," Reese said as soon as everyone had gotten a cup of coffee. "Here's the situation. CCC has a target for us—a reinforced NVA company that's being tracked by one of their RTs. It looks like they're headed in our direction, so we're going to see if we can't change their minds about fucking with us."

Santelli grinned broadly. This was his kind of operation—to get out there with enough force to put the enemy in the hurt locker for good. And, best of all, they would be hitting them first instead of sitting and waiting for an attack on the camp.

Reese traced a spot on the map with his pointer. "This is where our target is projected to be at approximately noon tomorrow. The RT tracking them will be in constant contact with us, so we can shift our position if they don't go exactly where we think they're going.

"One platoon will go in here," he said, tapping the map, "in a blocking position against this rise in the ground overlooking this clearing. A second platoon will be inserted behind the dinks so we can do a hammer-and-anvil number on them."

He glanced down at his notes. "CCC's got a battery of 175 mm Long Toms out of Firebase Rhonda laid on for us, as well as two Heavy Fire teams of Huey Hogs from the 269th—the Black Knights. They've been transferred up to Pleiku, so we'll be working together again."

There were several grins at the mention of the 269th Assault Helicopter Company. The Black Knights and their flamboyant leader, Major Butler, had done a

SOAR WITH THE EAGLE!

And in 1992, the Eagle flies even higher with more gripping adventure reading.

Introducing four new exciting miniseries that deliver action and adventure at a fast pace....

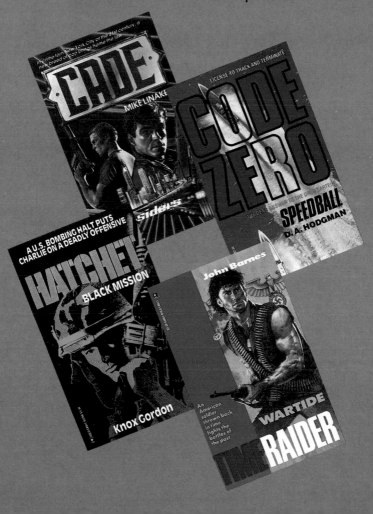

good job supporting A-410 on their last mission in Cambodia.

"Are there any questions so far?"

There were none.

"Santelli," Reese said, "I want you to take the hammer platoon with Kowalski, Wheeler and Hayes. I'll take the blocking force with Hotchkiss, Torres and Wilson." He turned to his team sergeant. "Sarge, that'll leave you, Rohm, Baker and Webb to hold the fort, but you'll have Third Platoon and we should be back by midafternoon."

"No sweat, sir," Pierce replied. "We can handle it."

"We're going to have to stay loose and play this by ear until the RT confirms exactly where they are, but once we've them spotted it should be pretty simple. Just hit them as hard as we can, inflict as many casualties as possible and then get the hell out of there." Reese looked around the bunker. "Any questions?"

Again there were none. The mission was straightforward and simple. Their job was to find the enemy and kill. Everyone had been through the drill enough times to make it second nature, and the fact that they would be going into Cambodia didn't make any difference. Only politicians worried about things like crossing supposedly neutral borders. To the Special Forces, war was war.

"Okay, then," Reese said, "let's get 'em ready to move out early tomorrow. Remember, the lift ships will be here at 0700." As the meeting broke up, Reese turned to Sergeant Pierce. "Guess who's the S-3 at CCC."

Pierce grinned. "I see you've met the Ice Man."

"Have you ever worked with him before?"

"We did a little number in Laos once back during the White Star days," Pierce recounted. "And I've never seen anyone as cold as that man. It'll be good working with him again because he doesn't miss a thing. If he's running the operation, you know we won't be left hanging like we were last month."

"That's good to know," Reese said. A-410's first impromptu mission for SOG had almost ended in a complete disaster because of a lack of planning on the part of the staff at SOG headquarters. "It'll be nice to work with a real professional for a change."

"You got that shit right, sir."

BACK IN HER APARTMENT Laura was busy getting ready for her return trip to Dak Sang. Now that she had a better idea of what the situation was at the remote border camp, she knew exactly what to pack for her trip. Nothing fancy, just durable field clothing and not even too much of that.

She planned to spend at least a week with Reese to get the story, so the first two things that went into her canvas bag were a couple of rolls of American-made toilet paper. Her previous visit to Dak Sang, as short as it had been, had taught her the true value of having enough toilet paper in the field, especially when the C-ration version felt like sandpaper.

As she packed, she added a few things to her bag that didn't fall into the absolute-necessities category. She had a feeling that Mike Reese might need a little softening up before she could get him to talk, so she added a black lace brassiere with matching bikini panties and a small bottle of perfume to her bag. Even at a primitive Special Forces camp it never hurt to smell like a woman, particularly since she was going to have to soothe a bruised male ego.

As soon as she was done, a quick phone call reserved her a seat on the morning Herky flight to Nha Trang, and she was all set to go. She had only to wait now, but that was hard. She had finally gotten permission to cover her first big story, and she was anxious to get working on it. Also, she had to admit that she wanted to see Reese again.

She was still of two minds about the Special Forces officer. She had vowed that until her career was firmly established she wasn't going to get involved with a man in any way that would prevent her from attaining her goals. Reese, however, was part of her goal this time, so she could relax and enjoy being with him. Nevertheless, she had made up her mind that she wouldn't allow him to get too firmly entrenched in her bed. As long as she didn't fall in love with him, she could enjoy their relationship. If it got in the way of her career, however, he would have to go.

Laura didn't feel like going out for dinner that evening, so she ate what the cook whipped up downstairs. The food at the villa wasn't bad—an interesting mixture of French, Vietnamese and American cuisine that she had grown used to. Tonight, though, she hardly noticed what she ate. She was keyed up over the prospect of finally getting to cover an important story, the beginning of her real journalistic career as she saw it, but there was no one in the villa she could talk to about the story. Marshall had made that more than clear to her during their meeting.

After dinner she went back up to her room and crawled into bed early. As she drifted off to sleep, she saw the raw red earth of the Dak Sang camp in her mind.

13

July 3, Dak Sang

At daybreak the two Nung platoons were formed up and waiting on the open ground in front of the command bunker when Reese appeared. The strikers were traveling light today, carrying only two days' rations and a double load of ammunition. Every M-60 machine gun Reese had dared to pull off the perimeter, however, had been added to reinforce their firepower.

If CCC's intelligence on the enemy unit was correct, they would be outnumbered at least two to one. But the element of surprise, the additional firepower and the artillery support would do a lot to even up the odds, and Reese wasn't overly concerned about the outcome. He knew the old truism that no battle plan ever survived the initial contact with the enemy. But if things went the way Major Snow had planned, they would make contact with the NVA, tear them a new asshole and be back to the camp before dark.

"What's the latest word, sir?" Santelli asked as he walked up. "Are we still on?" The XO was fully suited up for war this morning: tiger suit, Swedish K, face paint and all. Since he would be leading the tracking platoon, his ruck was packed light with little more than extra ammunition and water.

Reese grinned. "RT Ghost says they're on the move again and they're still keeping to their original course, straight for us, so the mission's a go."

Santelli grinned back. "We're really going to put them in the hurt locker this time, Captain."

"I sure as hell hope so," Reese agreed. "I'd much rather do it to them out there than wait for them to come in closer and do it to us here." Reese glanced at the Nungs. "What in the hell is Vao doing here?" he asked when he spotted the old Nung standing by the formation.

Santelli shrugged. "He said he was going out with us. What can I say?"

Reese knew better than to try to keep Vao from doing something when he had made his mind up. The old jungle fighter had probably gotten bored hanging around the camp and decided to see if he could stir up some trouble. "Okay," he sighed. "I'll take him with me."

"When's the lift coming in?" Santelli asked.

Reese checked the time. "Not long now. You'd better get 'em on down to the pad."

Just as Santelli turned to go, the first flight of four Huey slicks escorted by a Light Fire team of three UH-1C Huey Hog gunships appeared from the east.

"Let's go, people!" Santelli shouted. "Saddle up!"

As each of the slicks touched down on the pad, a squad of Nungs ran to clamber aboard. As soon as the Huey was full and lifted off in a flurry of dust, another one came down to take its place, and more strikers boarded.

Reese climbed into the back of the last ship, followed by Hotchkiss, and the door gunner handed him a spare flight helmet before he sat down. Jamming his camouflaged boonie hat into the side pocket of his tiger suit pants, he quickly put the helmet on and plugged the cord into the ship's intercom system. "We're a go back here," he called up to the pilot.

"Our ETA will be about twenty-five minutes," the pilot reported back as he hauled up on the collective pitch control to lift the heavily laden slick from the dirt pad. "Then we'll come back and pick up your other unit."

Reese shot the pilot a thumbs-up and looked forward through the canopy as the troop-carrying slicks joined up with their gunship escort for the short flight into Cambodia. There was nothing on the ground to indicate when they penetrated Cambodian airspace, but Reese knew that the end of the valley was some four klicks on the other side of the fence. The dense vegetation and rolling hills that passed under him looked exactly like the terrain on either side of the valley at Dak Sang, and there was no way to tell that they were flying over Cambodia instead of South Vietnam. The border was of more significance to politicians poring over their maps than it was to the men who were going to fight and die in the thick jungle below. It didn't really matter when you were dead whether you died in Cambodia or Vietnam.

As the flight approached the landing zone, Reese unbuckled his seat belt and went up to kneel behind the pilot's seat so that he could watch through the canopy. While the slicks stayed high out of the range of small-arms fire, the three UH-1C gunships dropped low over the clearing, trolling for fire. They didn't recon by fire this time, discharging their weapons into likely hiding places because it would only serve to alert the NVA about the air assault. But they visually checked the tree line closely to make sure Reese wasn't stepping out into an ambush.

When the gunship leader radioed that the LZ was green, Reese slipped the helmet off, pulled back on the charging handle to chamber a round in his CAR-15, flicked the weapon on safety and took his place with the Nungs in the open door. It was show time.

Two by two the slicks went in, their tails high as they flared out over the small clearing. No sooner had the pilots killed their forward momentum and touched their skids to the ground than the Nungs jumped out, quickly fanning out into the knee-high elephant grass to establish a quick defensive perimeter.

Looking over their shoulders to make sure everyone was out, the slick drivers quickly pulled pitch and lifted off. They had been on the ground for less than twenty seconds. The second pair of Hueys were right behind them, and Reese was through the door before the skids of his ship even touched down. He knelt in the tall grass, holding his boonie hat in place against the rotor blast.

In seconds the last two slicks were gone. It had been a prefect insertion: quick in, drop off the troops and get the hell out of there without anyone being the wiser. As soon as the beating of the rotors faded away, Reese got to his feet. Using arm and hand signals, he immediately sent out his flank and point security.

Hotchkiss went up with the point element, and after taking a quick compass reading, started off into the tree line to the west.

They only had a couple of klicks to go before reaching their planned ambush position, and Reese was content to move carefully. He was looking for someone to kill today, but he wanted to find the NVA unit himself rather than be found by them. Even with RT Ghost dogging their heels, he had to be careful he didn't stumble into the enemy's point elements before Santelli made his insertion behind them.

Since they were in Cambodia, Reese had Hotchkiss keep to the trails instead of breaking bush. The trails had been made by the North Vietnamese and, since they considered Cambodia to be their own backyard, they didn't booby-trap the trails the way they did in Vietnam. Even so it was still slow going in the thick jungle, and the point had to move cautiously in case another NVA unit was also in the area.

They had been on the march for a little under an hour when, right on schedule, Santelli's voice came in over the radio. "Bent Talon Six, this is Talon Five, over."

"This is Talon Six," Reese answered. "Go ahead."

"This is Talon Five. We're in position at 523903 and are ready to move out. How copy, over?"

"Talon Six, roger copy," Reese answered. "We're moving in on our location right now and we'll be waiting for you. Keep me informed. Out."

Reese handed the radio handset back to his Nung RTO and went up to join the point element. According to his calculations, they should be close to the small clearing he had chosen as his ambush site. He found Hotchkiss squatting at the edge of the trail on a slight rise in the ground overlooking the clearing. He slid in beside the sergeant and, pulling his field glasses from his rucksack, carefully scanned the area.

Reese had picked the ambush site from maps and recon photos, and fortunately it looked as good on the ground as it had in the photos. The clearing was a little more than a hundred yards across and a hundred and fifty deep. The trail they had been following, and the one the NVA would be taking, ran through the left-hand side of the open ground. From where he was he had a slight elevation advantage that provided good fields of fire over the entire clearing. It was a perfect spot for an ambush.

By now Vao had joined him, and the smile on his weathered face as he surveyed the clearing told Reese more about the terrain than anything he had seen. "Number one place, *Dai Uy*. We will kill many Cong here today."

If old Vao liked the ambush site, it had to be good. Using hand and arm signals, Reese sent the Nungs out to both flanks in an L-shaped formation with the long arm of the L to his left. Hotchkiss took the left and Torres the right while Reese stayed in the angle of the L with Vao and the radio.

Once everyone was in position, hidden well back in the trees, Reese got on the radio and reported their location to Dak Sang. Pierce would relay the information back to CCC at Kontoum. Next he made contact with the supporting 175 mm Long Tom battery at Firebase Rhonda and preplotted several artillery concentrations. Then he checked his magazines and lay down to wait. Now came the trying part of the operation—waiting for Santelli to drive the NVA to him.

SANTELLI HANDED the radio handset back to his Nung RTO and tightened the straps to his ruck. It was time for him to start earning his combat pay. They had made the insertion without being spotted, but that was only the beginning. The hard part was yet to come. He had to make contact with the rear of the enemy unit without being detected, and that might not be easy. The NVA kept a close eye on their backtrail and maintained their points well out to the front.

Also, to keep the NVA from detecting their insertion, they had been dropped several klicks behind the enemy formation. To catch up they needed to move quickly. Once they had caught up they had to follow the enemy, and, if necessary, take them under fire to drive them into Reese's trap.

One big thing in their favor was that since they were in Cambodia, the enemy wouldn't have booby-trapped the trails. The NVA rarely messed up their own backyard, and he would be able to advance as fast as the terrain allowed. Taking out his compass and map, Santelli took the point position himself so that he could set the pace.

In just under half an hour, Santelli stumbled onto the NVA's backtrail and started following it. Half a klick farther on he came to their camp of the previous night. The NVA was notorious for not policing up their campsites in Cambodia, and this one was no exception. The place looked like a small city dump.

Empty ration cans, cigarette packages, ammo packaging and garbage littered the site. He stepped up to the remnants of a small cook fire and, placing his hand in the ashes, found the spot still warm. They probably weren't more than a klick or so ahead, or in terms of time the enemy had a twenty-minute advantage.

After quickly combing through the debris, Santelli took up the point again and started down the trail. As he double-timed, he got on the horn to report to Reese. The captain rogered the message and told him to keep on until contact was made with the NVA rear guard.

Topping the next low ridge, Santelli caught a glimpse of movement around the bend of the trail five hundred yards in front of them. Motioning for Kowalski to stay a hundred yards behind with the platoon, Santelli sprinted on up the trail and around the bend. As soon as he reached the next straight stretch, he saw the NVA trail guard a hundred and fifty yards away.

The guard watching his unit's backtrail was real sloppy. His orders were to keep a couple of hundred yards behind the main body, but he had allowed the interval to lengthen out to twice that distance. He was strolling along, his head down and his AK-47 slung over his shoulder as if he thought he was the only human in that part of Cambodia. He was young, and Santelli figured he was a new recruit fresh down the Ho Chi Minh Trail from North Vietnam.

Santelli had a sudden idea. Turning around, he motioned Kowalski up to him and whispered softly.

Kowalski grinned and nodded. Motioning for Cowboy, his Nung interpreter, to come with him, Santelli slipped into the bush along the side of the trail.

14

July 3, Cambodia

Running through the bush as quietly as he could, Santelli reached around and pulled the silenced Ruger semiautomatic pistol with the telescopic sight from the side pocket of his ruck. Pulling back on the slide, he chambered a round and flicked the safety on. He carried the silenced pistol specifically for occasions like this—a silent kill. Sometimes he hunted wild game with it on long missions when the rations ran out, but mostly he used it to take out NVA sentries or trail guards.

When he felt he had run far enough, Santelli stepped out to the edge of the trail and looked eastward. His target was some ninety yards ahead, still walking along slowly as though he didn't have a care in the world. Even with the telescopic sight, the range was at the outer limits for accurate shooting with the Ruger, but Santelli was confident that he could make the long shot. Dropping into the bush at the edge of the trail, he took up a two-handed sitting position to fire.

As he sighted the silenced pistol on the back of the NVA's neck, he thought that the guy really should have paid more attention to his training classes on tactical movement in the jungle. He hadn't turned around to check his rear even once. But it was too late for that now. Santelli wasn't about to give the man a chance to learn from his mistake.

The Ruger barely made an audible pop, and the NVA slumped to his knees as the .22 round mushroomed in the base of his brain. He was dead before he fell forward on his face, his AK slipping off his shoulder as he hit the ground.

Santelli and Cowboy dashed down the trail, grabbed the body by the arms and dragged it into the bush. The NVA slack man was somewhere ahead out of sight, but they didn't want to take a chance on his coming back to check on what was keeping his comrade.

While Santelli stripped off the dead man's ammo carrier, bedroll and uniform shirt, the Nung ran back out to get his AK and pith helmet. It took only a second for Cowboy to change into the NVA's uniform and equipment. What little blood there was on the dark olive uniform shirt was all on the back and wouldn't be noticed. Wearing the NVA's pith helmet, chest riding magazine carrier and bedroll, the Nung could pass himself off as one of the enemy until someone got right up to him and saw his Mike Force boots.

Cowboy pulled back on the AK's charging handle to check the round in the chamber. Satisfied that the weapon was loaded, he flicked it off safety and stepped back out into the open. Holding the assault rifle at port arms, he hurried up the trail at double time. He wanted to get the NVA slack man in sight as soon as possible.

Kowalski had already brought up the rest of the platoon and, rejoining them, Santelli took off after

Cowboy as fast as he could. As he ran, he took the radio handset from the Nung RTO running beside him and put in another call to Reese. "Talon Six, this is Five." Santelli's voice was only a whisper over the radio as he told his commander that he had substituted the Nung for the NVA trail watch man. "We're right behind them now," he concluded, checking his map. "I estimate another five or ten minutes before they arrive at your location, over."

"Six, roger," Reese answered curtly. "Keep me informed. Out."

By now Santelli had Cowboy in sight again and halted the platoon alongside the trail. The Nung was walking at a fast pace, his AK held at the ready, when he suddenly slipped into the bush at the side of the trail and took cover. Santelli whipped out his field glasses and focused them on the interpreter. Using hand and arm signals, Cowboy told him that the North Vietnamese column was a hundred yards in front of him and was closing in on the clearing. Santelli reached for the radio handset.

"Six, this is Five," he radioed Reese. "Company's coming, Captain. Keep your heads down. Out."

FROM HIS HIDING PLACE at the base of a large tree where the trail led back into the jungle at the edge of the clearing, Reese watched the enemy point element move through the open toward him. The combination of the tiger suit and the camouflage face paint would make it difficult for anyone to spot him against the backdrop of foliage until they were right on top of him.

The NVA unit was moving fast, seemingly unconcerned that trouble might be lying in wait in the jungle. After all, they were still safe in their Cambodian sanctuary where the American President didn't allow his Army to go in after them. Letting the North Vietnamese operate unhindered in Cambodia and Laos was a military blunder unparalleled in the history of modern warfare, but the NVA weren't complaining about it. But they also seemed to have forgotten that MACV-SOG fought their war by a different set of rules.

As soon as Reese could see the lead elements of the enemy column, he picked up the radio handset. "Red Leg Five Niner, this is Bent Talon Six," he radioed to the artillery FDC. "Fire mission, over."

"This is Red Leg Five Niner," the artillery FDC called back. "Send it."

"This is Talon Six. Fire concentration Bravo, troops in the open, range three hundred yards, HE VT, will adjust, over."

"This is Five Niner. Good copy, wait out."

A few seconds later the FDC was back. "Talon Six, this is Five Niner. Shot over."

"This is Six. Shot out," Reese replied, waiting for the characteristic sound of a rushing freight train as the 175 mm shell flashed overhead.

"This is Five Niner. Slash, over."

High in the sky a small black cloud burst into life. The shell had burst so high over their heads that the NVA only looked up in surprise, as if trying to figure out what it was. It had been set to burst that high for a reason, and served its purpose. Reese could see where the artillery was aimed, but it hadn't spooked the enemy the way a ground burst would have.

"Five Niner, this is Talon Six," he radioed. "Splash. Repeat range, fire for effect, over."

"Five Niner, on the way, wait."

This time the sound of six freight trains was heard as all six of the long-range guns in the battery fired at the same time.

"Splash, over," the FDC called as soon as the shells detonated two hundred yards in the air over the heads of the NVA. Reese had called for VT fusing on the projectiles, a radar proximity fusing that caused them to detonate at a certain altitude above the ground and rain hundreds of red-hot shards of razor-sharp shrapnel onto the target. There was no shelter from air-burst artillery short of a bunker with a reinforced roof.

The effect of the airbursts on the NVA caught out in the open was disastrous. Reese saw most of the men at the front of the column cut down by the shrapnel. He knew the trees would have provided some protection for the enemy troops who hadn't reached the clearing yet, but not much.

There was a long pause while the artillerymen back at the fire base rammed fresh projectiles and powder bags into their long-range weapons, then the deadly black bursts again appeared over the edge of the clearing. This time, however, as soon as the shells burst, the NVA got to their feet and ran. Even with the casualties they had sustained in the first volley, though, the NVA unit was disciplined. Rather than break up into a screaming mob running through the jungle, they tried to get through the artillery barrage and reach safety on Reese's side of the clearing.

Hidden back in the trees the Nungs waited until the enemy were only twenty yards away before they opened up with a withering storm of small-arms fire. The NVA stopped dead in their tracks. Rather than retreat into the artillery barrage, however, they took what cover there was in the tall grass and returned fire.

Caught in the open between the artillery and Reese's men, the North Vietnamese started maneuvering. The group that was still under the rain of artillery split off from the main body and disappeared into the jungle on each side of the clearing. Suddenly Reese heard the high-pitched chatter of M-16s and the answering heavier hammering of AKs on his left flank as Hotchkiss and his Nungs took them under fire.

Then he realized what the enemy commander's strategy was. The NVA were trying to get in close enough to Reese's position so that the artillery couldn't shoot for fear of hitting the friendlies.

Now that most of the North Vietnamese had moved out of the artillery impact area, Reese called the FDC to adjust the artillery fire in closer to support Hotchkiss. "Red Leg Five Niner, this is Talon Six. Left one-fifty, drop one-fifty, fire for effect, over."

There was a short pause while the FDC calculated the adjustment. "Bent Talon Six, this is Five Niner," the FDC radioed. "Your last adjustment brings you into Danger Close situation. Please advise, over."

Danger Close artillery fire was an adjustment that would bring the artillery rounds in to impact less than two hundred yards from the friendly positions. The long-range 175 mm guns were accurate, but not accurate enough to fire Danger Close at this extreme range. There was too great a risk of a short round falling on the friendly positions. It was time to call on the gunships to give them a hand.

"Five Niner, this is Talon Six. Roger Danger Close, end of mission, over."

"This is Red Leg Five Niner. Copy end of fire mission. Good Luck. Out."

The last round that burst over the clearing exploded in a billowing white cloud instead of the black burst of the earlier rounds. It was a Willie Pete shell, white phosphorus, to signal the end of the fire mission.

Now that the artillery had stopped taking its deadly toll the NVA quickly reorganized. Realizing that the American unit was a serious threat, the North Vietnamese commander decided to take them out rather than slip away into the jungle and try to bypass them.

Reese heard the volume of enemy fire on his left increase and knew that it wasn't over yet. He was going to have to fight this thing out on the ground until he could get the Black Knights in. The first priority was to get Santelli and his platoon in on the left flank to take the pressure off Hotchkiss.

Santelli had already started moving his platoon toward the sound of the contact, and Reese could hear the firing in the background over the radio when Santelli answered. "We're moving in on them now," the lieutenant said. "But you'd better get those gunships in here ASAP. There's more of them than we can handle, over."

"Six, roger. I'll get right on that. Out."

"Black Snake, Black Snake," Reese radioed after he switched over to the CCC frequency. "This is Bent Talon Six. The NVA have moved in too close to use the arty and they're swarming all over us. Request gunship support ASAP, over."

"Black snake, roger," the CCC radio operator at Kontoum answered calmly. "We'll get 'em coming, Talon. You just hang in there, over."

"This is Six, roger. Out." Reese handed the handset back to the RTO, flicked the thumb safety on his CAR-15 over to rock and roll, full-automatic fire, and tapped the bottom of the magazine to make sure it was locked in place. So far the NVA were only pressing him on the left, but it wouldn't be long before they hit him, too.

RT Ghost had reported that the enemy unit was a reinforced infantry company, but they had failed to say just how much they had been reinforced. Instead of facing the eighty to a hundred troops he had been expecting, Reese quickly estimated that there were more than a hundred and forty men in the enemy unit. That was entirely too high a number for his two small Nung platoons to handle.

He quickly called both Hotchkiss and Torres, with an order to start pulling their troops back toward him to form a defensive circle. Until he could get the gunships in to reinforce their firepower they were going to be badly outnumbered.

Usually it took some time to get gunships onstation, but Major Snow had anticipated this problem, and the Black Knights were standing by at Kontoum on ramp alert instead of being at their home station at Pleiku. They should be overhead in just a little under fifteen minutes, but that might be the longest fifteen minutes of Reese's life.

The shrill blast of signal whistles sounded over the rattle of small-arms fire, and the NVA charged Reese's position. The Nungs had the advantage of cover and concealment, but they were vastly outnumbered and the enemy was determined to break through the ambush.

Reese spotted movement to his front and cut loose with a long burst of 5.56 mm. The M-60 to his left opened up, too, the bright orange-red tracers cutting across the elephant grass at the edge of the clearing.

15

July 3, Cambodia

To his left Reese saw Vao rise to one knee. Switching his M-16 over to semiautomatic fire, the Nung calmly started firing one round after another, picking his targets carefully as if he were on a firing range. Each time he fired, an NVA fell over dead or wounded. The old jungle fighter had a slight smile on his face as he dropped back down to change magazines. He enjoyed killing Communists.

The Nung machine gunner at Vao's side was rapping out accurate, controlled six-round bursts when the NVA concentrated on taking him out of action. First the M-60's loader took an AK round high in the chest. A second later a Chicom stick grenade arced through the air and detonated a few feet from the gunner, silencing the deadly fire. When he slumped over the breech of his gun, a young Nung rifleman raced to get the weapon back into action. Rolling his wounded comrades out of the way, he snatched up the gun and, resting the buttstock against his hip, screamed his war cry and let loose.

Under the accurate fire of Vao's rifle and the almost solid stream of 7.62 mm from the M-60, the NVA charge faltered, broke and was turned back, leaving several bodies lying in the grass.

Reese could hear the NVA whistles signaling for another attack when he dropped back down behind his tree and hit the magazine release to drop the empty from the magazine well of his CAR. He was pulling a fresh magazine from his ammo pouch when he heard the voice of Major Butler, the CO of the 269th Assault Helicopter Company, over the radio handset clipped to his assault harness.

"Bent Talon Six, Bent Talon Six," the pilot called. "This is Black Knight Lead on your push, over."

Reese slammed the fresh magazine into the CAR and pulled back on the charging handle to chamber a round before reaching for the radio. Over the rattle of the small-arms fire he heard the welcome sound of Huey rotors beating the air. With the gunship's help he might be able to get the situation back under control.

"This is Bent Talon Six," he called back. "'Bout time you guys got here, Black Knight. How 'bout lending us a hand down here? We're up to our asses in dinks."

"Roger, Talon Six. I've got a Heavy Fire team up here. Just tell me where you want us to put it."

"This is Six. You can start a hundred yards in front of my position. Make your runs from north to south and you'll be paralleling my front, over."

"Lead, roger. Pop smoke on your flanks."

"Roger Lead, wait one."

Reese yelled out for Hotchkiss and Torres to throw out smoke grenades. A second later two columns of colored signal smoke billowed up into the air.

"Lead, this is Talon Six. Smoke out."

"This is Lead, roger. I've got goofy grape on the right and cherry on the left."

"Roger red and purple. Go for it, Black Knight. They're tearing us up down here."

"Ya'll keep your heads down, you hear?" Butler's southern accent always intensified when he was going in hot. "We're rolling in now!"

The gunship pilot switched the radio over to aircraft frequency. "Two Seven, this is Lead. Cover my ass. I'm going in."

"Two Seven, roger."

"This is Lead. The rest of you spot your targets for the second run."

A chorus of "rogers" followed as Butler flicked on his arming switches, twisted his throttle all the way up against the stop and pulled pitch for maximum lift. "You ready?" He looked over at "Surfer Joe" Hawkins, his gunner.

Hawkins tightened his fingers around his firing controls, leaned forward to peer through his foldout gunsight and nodded. Butler nudged down on the rudder pedals to line up with the smoke markers and pushed forward on the cyclic control. The heavily armed gunship dropped out of the sky like a stone.

In Two Seven, the number two ship behind Butler, the warrant officer pilot took up a position five hundred yards behind and off to the right of his flight leader as he started down for his run. Black Knight Lead was known for cutting things a little too close, and from there he could cover Butler when he swept down over the enemy positions.

On the ground Reese and his men cheered when they saw the two Huey Hogs drop out of the sky. The NVA fire slackened as the enemy got ready to greet the gunships. They knew that if they wanted to survive, they had to knock the choppers out of the sky.

From a thousand yards out Hawkins started triggering off 2.75-inch rockets from his side-mounted pylons. Trailing dirty white smoke, the HE rockets raced toward the jungle in pairs. As the diving gunship drew closer, the red-and-white shark's mouth on the nose of the Huey blossomed flame as the gunner switched over to the 40 mm automatic Thumper in the nose turret. With its characteristic chunking sound the short-barreled Thumper spit its small, deadly fragmentation rounds down into the trees.

The rockets impacted with angry red-and-black bursts from the exploding HE warheads. Smaller puffs of black smoke appeared in between the rocket bursts when the 40 mm Thumper grenades detonated.

It was a seemingly endless hail of fire, but it didn't make the NVA keep their heads down. As Butler swept in closer, they fired everything they had at the diving gunship. The woods blazed with AK and RPD machine-gun fire. Lines of green tracer fire flashed up into the gunship's path. The pilot kicked down on his rudder pedals, snapping the ship's tail from side to side, trying to throw the enemy's aim off. But he heard and felt his ship take hits.

Suddenly Butler was past the target and in the clear. A quick check of his instruments showed that everything was still in the green as he stomped down on the right rudder pedal and slammed the cyclic control over to the side to bring his chopper around again as fast as he could. The heavily laden Huey shuddered in the air as it skidded into the turn. He knew better than to try that kind of turn so close to the ground, but he had no choice. He had to get back to take the heat off Two Seven.

Five hundred yards behind him Two Seven had already started his gun run. In the left-hand seat the gunner triggered the rocket pods hanging off the pylons on the sides of the ship. The 2.75-inch HE rockets shot out of the pods in pairs and raced toward their target. The jungle exploded in front of them.

Ahead of Two Seven, Butler pulled up out of his gun run. Now the NVA could concentrate all their fire on his wingman. Two Seven's gunner hunched lower in his armored seat as he peered through his gunsight and triggered his weapons. He was very glad he was wearing his chicken plate ceramic-armored vest today.

The gunship swept on down even closer as the deadly streams of green tracer fire switched from concentrating on Butler's gunship to shooting at him. Shifting over to the automatic 40 mm grenade launcher mounted in the Huey's nose turret, Two Seven's gunner pressed the trigger, swinging the Thumper from side to side and spraying grenades into the jungle. He wasn't even trying to be accurate, because all he wanted to accomplish was to divert the enemy's attention so that he wouldn't be shot out of the sky.

Two Seven was two hundred yards out when the NVA decided to get serious. The first thing they did was to shoot the ship full of holes.

Butler was completing his low-level turn to bring his gunship screaming down again. The first thing he saw was his wingman taking heavy fire. "Two Seven!" the pilot shouted over the radio. "Get your ass outta there!"

The Huey staggered back up into the air, followed by lines of green tracer fire. By this time the other three gunships had picked their own targets and were diving to add their firepower to the melee, but they were out of position to help Two Seven. It was up to Butler to go to his wingman's aid.

The Southerner kicked down on his rudder pedals, and the gunship's nose skidded to the left, lining him up on the glowing green fire coming up out of the trees. In the chopper's left-hand seat Surfer Joe zeroed his gunsight in on the heaviest source of enemy fire and triggered the pylon-mounted quad M-60s. Even with the burst limiters holding down the amount of ammunition going through the four weapons the rain of fire they put out was impressive. The combined impact of so many bullets at once shredded the jungle. Anything smaller than a tree was instantly pulped.

For the first time the enemy fire on Two Seven slackened. The pilot was able to get his Hog turned around and was climbing back into the sky. "Knight Lead, this is Two Seven," he radioed. "We've taken hits, and I'm getting a little turbine surge. We're heading back to the barn while I can still keep her in the air.''

"Roger, Two Seven," Butler radioed. "Switch over to search-and-rescue push and check in with them, over."

"This is Two Seven, roger. I'm switching over now."

"Good luck, Two Seven," Butler called as he watched the crippled ship slowly bank away to the east and the Vietnamese border. "Lead out."

With Two Seven safely heading home it was time to get back to work. The other three gunships were working as a team, covering one another as they made their runs against a heavy source of fire on the northern edge of the clearing. As Butler watched, a machine gun on the other side of the clearing suddenly opened up on the Hogs, and the Black Knight captain went into action again.

"Heads up back there!" he called out on the intercom to the two door gunner loaders in the back of the ship. "We're going in!"

The door gunners leaned out into the slipstream, their 60s hammering out long bursts as Butler dived again. With a whoosh rockets leaped from the side pods and streaked for the jungle. The smoke from their launch obscured the door gunners' targets for a second, and they backed off their triggers.

As the gunship swept in over the edge of the clearing, Hawkins swung the Thumper turret over to the right side and continued spitting rounds. The left-side door gunner saw dark uniformed figures in the trees raising their rifles as the gunship flashed overhead. He brought his M-60 to bear and gave them a long, sustained burst. He was right on target, and he saw the enemy go down.

Butler's run, however, hadn't taken out the machine gun. Green tracer fire chased him back up into the sky as he climbed out. He kicked his ship around again in a sharply banked turn, and the airframe shuddered as the rotors unloaded and lost lift. He was very close to stalling out and crashing in the jungle, but at the last moment the pilot rolled out, dropped the nose to regain his airspeed and swept back down on the target.

This time he came in directly at them, right down the muzzle of the weapon. It was a dangerous practice to overfly a machine-gun position after the gun run. If you didn't take it out, it had an easy belly shot at you. But coming in dead-on gave him a better shot. The door gunners saw what he was doing and braced themselves. When the gunship flew back over the tree line, it would be up to them to keep the enemy down until they were clear.

Butler kicked the Huey from side to side as Surfer Joe fired the rockets, spreading them in a shotgun pattern. The jungle came apart with the explosions. Dirt, broken tree limbs and pieces of smashed men flew up into the air.

The door gunners started firing even before they were over the target. Solid streams of red tracers reached down into the smoke-filled jungle. The speeding ship whooshed over the tree line, and the gunners swung out on their lifelines, keeping their guns on target as they swept overhead. This time no more fire came from that position.

On the ground Reese's men were making their own contribution to the slaughter. As the NVA tried to run from the gunships, the Nung riflemen stood up and carefully put bullets into their backs.

The barrels of the Nungs' M-60s glowed dull red as the linked ammunition belts rattled through the feed trays of the guns. The gunners laid back hard on their triggers without pausing to cool the breeches or to conserve ammunition. They had so many targets that the edge of the clearing resembled a shooting gallery.

The M-79 grenadiers, however, picked their targets more carefully before firing. They were low on ammunition and wanted to make every last 40 mm grenade count, and count they did. Each dirty black puff of smoke of an exploding grenade sent at least one NVA sprawling to the ground.

16

July 3, Cambodia

When Butler pulled up into the sky again, he circled the clearing, waiting for the smoke to drift away. The other three gunships hovered protectively above him, the gunners scanning the jungle for more targets. But for now there was nothing worth shooting at. Finally Butler got tired of waiting and dropped out of the sky once more, bringing his ship screaming down low over the tree line as close as he could, trolling for fire.

But nothing moved in the edge of the clearing. At last it seemed as though the North Vietnamese had decamped for places unknown. But wherever they had gone they had sure as hell learned that it wasn't healthy to shoot at Black Knight gunships.

After one last low pass over the smoking jungle, the five gunships climbed back into the sky. "Talon Six, this is Black Knight Lead," Butler called down to Reese. "We're bingo ammo and are heading back to the barn. A Light Fire team is standing by if you need any more help, over."

"Talon, roger," Reese called back. "Thanks for the assist, Black Knight. It was much appreciated."

"This is Lead. *De nada,* Talon. That's what we're here for, but you owe us another party."

Reese chuckled. "Roger that, Black Knight. You bring the broads again and we'll supply the booze."

"That's a big rog, Talon." Butler laughed. "Black Knight. Out."

When the beat of the gunship rotors faded in the distance, Reese called Santelli and ordered his platoon to move out and sweep the area to the west of the battle scene. The surviving NVA would be fading back into the jungle as fast as they could to regroup and lick their wounds, but there was still a chance to catch up with some of them and make their lives a little more miserable.

While Santelli's platoon took off through the woods, Reese's people policed up the battlefield. The NVA dead were stripped of their weapons and ammunition and quickly searched for documents or any other information about their unit's identity. Since the North Vietnamese usually didn't wear unit insignia like the American Army, documents and individual paybooks were often the only clue as to who they were up against. CCC would go over what they found and try to match it up with their other order of battle information.

While the medics were working on the wounded Nungs, Reese called in the Dust-off chopper to take out the seriously wounded. Normally the Dust-offs didn't fly into Cambodia, but CCC had arranged for one of their Black Ops Medevac birds to stand by in case it was needed. By the time the first Dust-off arrived Reese had the casualty report. Only two strikers were dead, but four more were seriously wounded and another half a dozen had received minor wounds that didn't require hospitalization. None of the Americans had been hit.

Twenty-two enemy bodies had been counted, but thirty-nine individual weapons had been captured, so Reese knew several more must have been seriously wounded. Along with the AK and SKS assault rifles they had also captured three 7.62 mm RPD machine guns and an RPG rocket launcher. All told, the battlefield salvage proved that they had eliminated at least one NVA platoon completely and had inflicted serious damage on the rest of the company. Not too bad for an afternoon's work.

As soon as the Dust-off lifted off and headed for the hospital at Kontoum, Reese called Santelli and told him to break off his pursuit. The lieutenant wanted to keep tracking, but CCC didn't want them in Cambodia any longer than was absolutely necessary. It was time to call for the lift ships to take them back across the fence.

MIKE REESE WAS TIRED but jubilant when he stepped off the Huey slick back at the Dak Sang camp. The mission had been more than merely successful; it had been textbook perfect. With the help of the Black Knights' aerial firepower, they had done a thorough job on the NVA company while suffering only minimum casualties themselves. Now maybe they would get some peace for a while so that they could get the camp finished.

Leaving Santelli to take care of standing down the troops and making sure the Nung walking wounded got to the dispensary, Reese headed straight for his CP to check in with Sergeant Pierce and write up his after-action report for CCC. When he stepped down into the command bunker, he was stunned to see Laura Winthrop waiting for him.

"What in hell are you doing here again?" he exploded.

"Before you say anything," she said quickly, handing him an envelope, "please read this."

Parking his weapon and ruck against the wall, he tore open the envelope bearing his name and rank on the front. Inside was a single sheet of paper and, glancing at the top, he saw Marshall's name with a Tan Son Nhut AFB building number as an address. The curt letter ordered Reese to show Laura every courtesy and to answer any questions she asked about his unit and his operations. He read the letter through twice before putting it back in the envelope and tucking it away in his pocket.

"I don't know how you managed to do this," he said, slowly shaking his head. "But obviously you did and so now you can get your story."

"Are you mad at me?"

Reese looked at her. "Mad?" He shook his head again. "No, but I've got a real bad feeling I'm going to regret your being here before this is all over. Colonel Marshall's going to tear me a new asshole, because he's going to think I put you up to this."

"Oh, no, he won't," she replied quickly. "I was able to convince him that you had nothing to do with my learning about the infamous Studies and Observations Group."

"How in hell did you manage to do that?"

She smiled. "I ratted on the guys who did, some of the reporters who've been here a long time."

"Jesus! That's going to make you real popular around the news desk."

"I'm not doing this to be popular," she said, her voice serious. "I'm just trying to get a story, a real story for a change instead of the shit I've been writing."

"Before we get too carried away here," Reese said, "you won't mind if I talk to my headquarters first and make sure they know about this? They're a little touchy about reporters."

"No." She smiled. "Not at all. If you'd like, I'll wait outside so you have a little privacy."

"Please," he replied, "I won't be but a moment."

Five minutes later Reese walked up the steps from the bunker to find Laura standing by the mortar pits talking to Santelli.

She flashed him a warm look when he walked up. "Did they say I was legit?"

"Yes," he admitted. "They said you're authorized to be here and that I can talk to you, but even they don't know how you did it. What did you do, anyway? Catch old Marshall coming out of the wrong whorehouse, the one offering fat young boys at discount prices?"

She laughed. "No, I just caught him between a security rock and a First Amendment hard place."

"Okay," Reese said. "It's your show, so where do you want to start?"

Laura didn't miss the note of resignation in his voice and decided to try to mend her fences before going any further with the interview. She wanted the story, but she didn't want to ruin the first blossoming of a promising relationship between them. Laura had to admit that it had been a long time since any of her relationships had offered much more than a quick roll in the sack and a nervous handshake in the morning.

When she graduated from college, she had expected she would have to put her professional life first if she wanted to make her mark as a journalist. But she hadn't realized the true cost of doing that. It wasn't that she lacked for male companionship in Vietnam. The problem was that most of her dates were either scared off when they learned about her job or they figured her for a quick trip to bed because she was a reporter.

Now that she had finally found a man she really enjoyed spending time with she didn't want to jeopardize that relationship. The story always came first, but maybe just this once she could have her story and Mike Reese, too, if she played her cards right.

"I'll tell you what," she said. "I could really use a cup of coffee and then maybe we could talk for a while before we get too serious. I don't want you to think I'm being pushy about this."

Reese hesitated. "I've got to talk to Pierce for a moment first."

Santelli stepped up to take over. "I can take Miss Winthrop over to the mess hall, Captain," he said, "and keep her entertained till you can join us. Don't worry," he added when Reese hesitated. "I won't tell her any of your secrets."

Reese laughed. "Okay, Jack. I'll join you as soon as I can."

"Right this way," Santelli said, taking Laura's arm. "Our cook's a Nung, but he does a decent cup of coffee."

LAURA SAT ACROSS the raw wooden table from Santelli with an Army-issue brown plastic coffee cup in her hands. The engineers had knocked together several tables and benches for the camp's mess hall from two-by-fours and plywood. Like the rest of the camp she had seen, the furnishings were crude but serviceable.

"Mike's pretty mad at me about this, isn't he?" she asked Santelli.

The XO shrugged. "You've got to understand the captain's position in this, Miss Winthrop."

"Laura, please."

"Okay, Laura," Santelli replied. "I'm Jack."

"What is his position? I really want to know."

"As I'm sure you've figured out by now," Santelli patiently explained, "this is one of the most classified operations in all of Southeast Asia. Anything you decide to write about us is going to get somebody hurt. And when that happens, Mike's going to be blamed for it. As they say in the Army, 'shit runs downhill,' and he's standing at the bottom of the hill on this."

Laura frowned. "But he's been ordered to answer my questions. Colonel Marshall said that it was okay for him to talk to me."

"That's not the way it really works, Laura," Santelli replied, turning the brown plastic cup around in his hands. "All the colonel's order means is that now he has someone to blame if the shit hits the fan. If anything goes wrong because of this story, it'll be the end of the captain's career. He'll spend the rest of his tour policing up cigarette butts in the rest stops along the Ho Chi Minh Trail."

"But I don't understand," Laura said. "Just a month ago he invited me to come up to your Ban Phoc camp and see how well the Special Forces war was going. Why did he do that if he knew it would get him into trouble?"

"It would have been okay for you to come to Ban Phoc. Back then we were a regular Special Forces Mike Force unit." He leaned closer to her to emphasize his point. "You've got to understand, Laura. We're not a Special Forces unit anymore. We're working for MACV-SOG now. We still wear the green beret, but we're not assigned to the Special Forces."

"But I don't understand—"

"And I can't explain it to you," Santelli cut in. "You're going to have to talk to him about it."

"That's okay." She took another sip of coffee. "Can you tell me anything about your mission, then? What are you doing up here so far away from any other units?"

"That's simple," he answered. "We're guarding the border to keep the NVA from moving more troop units into Vietnam during the so-called peace talks in Paris."

Laura frowned. "But according to the news releases I've seen, the North Vietnamese are limiting their movements while the talks are going on. They promised they'd do that in exchange for Johnson's bombing halt."

Santelli laughed. "They're moving more people across the border now than they did even before Tet. All the bombing halt has done is make it easier for them."

"How do you know? Where do you get your information?"

Santelli paused for a moment. "I'd better not answer that. That's another question you'll have to ask the captain. Can I get you a refill?" he asked, trying to put an end to her questions.

Laura looked around to see if Reese was showing up, but he was nowhere in sight. "Sure," she sighed. There was really nothing else she could do until he came back.

17

July 3, Dak Sang

Reese was still talking to Sergeant Pierce when Torres stuck his head out of the bunker. "Hey, Captain!" he shouted. "We've got some more visitors coming!"

Reese looked up at the sky.

"No!" Torres yelled, pointing down toward the camp gate. "They're coming up the road."

Reese turned around, looked eastward and saw a faint plume of red dust rising from the mouth of the valley. Who in hell would risk driving down that road when they could just as easily fly?

But the dust plume drew closer, and he saw the reason for the ground convoy. The lead vehicle was the dark, hulking shape of an M-48A-3 Patton medium tank. Following the lead tank was a jeep with yet another tank trailing behind it. It was a small convoy to be driving through Indian country, but having the tank's heavy firepower made up for its lack of size.

The M-48's turrets with their 90 mm main guns were slowly traversing from side to side, carefully checking the likely places where an RPG launcher might be hidden in ambush. Tanks had thick skins, but a single RPG antitank rocket in the right place could still ruin a tanker's whole day.

Reese started walking down to the gate to meet his unexpected visitors. He had no idea what the tanks were doing up here, but he'd find out soon enough. This could only be another one of Marshall's little schemes and, if the colonel was concerned enough to send armor to reinforce Dak Sang, Reese wondered what Marshall knew that he wasn't passing on. He was almost afraid to find out.

Reese was waiting down at the gate when the lead tank bearing the red-stained white number thirteen on the turret and the name Assassin on the main gun tube drove up. The driver locked his tracks, and the M-48 clanked to a halt alongside the road. The dust-covered tanker in the turret's TC hatch lifted his goggles and snapped a command down to the driver. With a bellow of black smoke from its multifuel engine the forty-seven-ton fighting machine pivoted on its treads so that its gun faced the jungle-covered hills to the south of the camp.

When the driver shut his engine down, the tank commander took off his CVC helmet, hung it on the .50-caliber machine gun and climbed down from his turret to the front slope of the tank hull. Reese could make out the faint outlines of subdued captain's bars sewn on the collar of the tanker's dusty, sweat-stained flak jacket.

"You the guy in charge around here?" the tanker asked.

Reese stepped up to the tank and extended his hand. "Mike Reese, Team A-410."

The tanker crouched on the hull to reach out and shake his hand. "Captain Ian Dublin of the Sixty-ninth Armor at your service. Where do you want us?"

Reese was taken aback. "No one told me you were coming."

"This is the Special Forces camp at Dak Sang, isn't it?"

"Yes, but—"

"Then this is the right place," Dublin said. Turning around, he grabbed his CVC helmet, spoke briefly into the radio mike and then hung it back on the machine gun. The second tank, bearing the number eleven and the name Asskicker, pulled up and took up a position on the other side of the road facing north. The jeep drove on inside the perimeter wire and braked to a stop.

"This is what's left at First Platoon, Alpha Company, out of Firebase Linda," Dublin announced. "And as soon as I get the other two First Platoon tanks put back together, I'll get them up here for you, too." The commander of the second tank climbed down and walked over to Reese and Dublin. "This is Sergeant Miles," Dublin explained, "my First Platoon leader. He'll be your point of contact for our operation up here after I leave."

The sergeant wiped a dirty hand on his even dirtier fatigues before offering it to Reese.

"Just exactly what is your operation supposed to be?" Reese asked. "No one said a thing to me about any tanks working in this area."

Dublin shook his head. "All I know is that I was given orders to get these cans up here as fast as I could for a camp defense mission."

"Where'd these orders come from?"

"Beats the shit outta me." Dublin shrugged. "The S-3 snatched me away from the club and told me to get a platoon up here ASAP." He looked out into the jungle around the hilltop. "Apparently someone thinks you're in deep kimchi up here."

Reese didn't know who exactly had given the order, but he had a pretty good idea where it had originated. "Did this movement order happen to come down with a hot shit priority on it?"

"Of course it did," Dublin said. "Why in hell do you think I came all the way up here myself? I'm supposed to be the company commander of this mob, not some fucking 'butter bar' platoon leader."

"Look," Reese said, "why don't you and your sergeant come over to my command bunker so we can talk about this. I might even be able to scrounge up a couple of cold beers for you and your people."

Dublin spit on the ground. "I'd kiss a pig's ass for a cold beer right now."

Reese grinned. "I don't think we've got a pig handy, but would a crusty old Green Beret team sergeant do?"

Dublin guffawed. "Bring him on."

AFTER GETTING DUBLIN and his tankers settled down in the command bunker with their beer, Reese found Laura in the mess hall listening to more of Santelli's stories of derring-do in the Green Berets.

"Laura," he said, "I just had a couple of tanks show up and I need to get them settled down for the night. So I'm going to leave you in Santelli's capable hands a little longer while I get this taken care of. If there's anything you want to know about the Nungs or the Mike Force, he can actually tell you more about them than I can."

Laura was disappointed, but she knew he did have to take care of business first. "Okay, I'll get Jack to show me around until you're done."

"This shouldn't take more than an hour or so." Reese went off to handle the most important task, which was getting the M-48s integrated into the camp's defenses. He found Dublin finishing off his second can of beer by the command bunker.

"You about ready to put us to work?" the tanker asked, crushing the empty can against a sandbag.

"I've never worked with tanks before," Reese said. "So I'm open to suggestions on the best way for us to use your firepower."

Dublin looked around the small hill with a professional eye. "Well, tanks really aren't supposed to be used as pillboxes, but since we're stuck up here, we need to get our hulls underground before dark."

"Underground? What do you mean?"

"RPGs," Dublin explained. "Our hull armor is thickest in the front, but sitting stationary in the open here, we're an easy target for an RPG through the belly where we're pretty thin. In order to protect ourselves we need to dig a position in the dirt so that only our turrets are aboveground. The turrets are eleven inches thick, but the sides of the hull are only a little over two inches and, if we get hit there, an RPG warhead can punch through that like it was cardboard."

Like most infantrymen, Reese believed that tanks were almost impregnable and didn't fully realize how vulnerable they could be to infantry antitank weapons. "I've got an engineer team up here with us, and they've got a small bulldozer. Let's go see their CO, and you can tell him what you need."

It was only a matter of fifteen minutes or so for the engineers' bulldozer to scrape out two primary firing positions, facing west, for Dublin's M-48s. While the bulldozer was at it, Dublin had it dig two more secondary positions, as well, one covering the north slope of the hill and one the south.

As soon as the primary firing positions were finished, Dublin and Sergeant Miles ground-guided the two tanks into the holes. When the front ends of the tanks were below the level of the ground, the gunners checked to make sure the turrets had clearance to traverse a full 360 degrees.

"There," Dublin said, "that ought to do it. Now you have two 90 mm pillboxes with power turrets. And, with the cupola .50 and the 7.62 co-ax gun, you've got a lot of firepower on call here. If anyone fucks with you, they won't live to regret it."

Now that the tanks were in place the crews climbed up on their rear decks and pulled their duffel bags out of the racks on the rear of the turrets to start setting up housekeeping. In seconds lean-tos appeared, sleeping bags were laid out under the tanks, and a small gas stove was heating water for coffee and hot rations.

Reese was impressed. "Your people are pretty good at making themselves at home."

"They have to be," Dublin replied dryly. "They live in those fucking cans. We don't see our base camp more than a couple of days a month."

"Is there anything I can get for them?" Reese asked.

Dublin thought for a moment. "Well, the men will sleep with the cans," he said. "And except for food and water they have just about everything they need with them. We will need some diesel fuel for the vehicles tomorrow, however—about a hundred gallons. Also a little fifty-weight oil—a couple of cases. And," he added, "we could sure use a refill on the beer."

Reese grinned. "I'll order the diesel and oil to be sent up with the morning resupply bird, but I can handle the beer right now."

The tanker grinned broadly. "I knew there was something I liked about this place."

Dick Clifford was in the MACV-SOG radio room when the after-action report of Reese's contact came in from CCC. He quickly read through it, whistling softly to himself when he noted the North Vietnamese body count. Reese had had himself a busy day, and Marshall was going to be tickled pink to see this. Maybe he'd be so happy that he would let Clifford leave early so he could make his poolside date at the Circle Sportief. He doubted it, but it was worth a try. He signed for the classified document, put it in an envelope and started upstairs with it.

Marshall was pleased with the report, so pleased, in fact, that he turned around in his swivel chair and, taking two glasses from the oak bar behind his desk, filled them with brandy from a decanter and handed one to Clifford. The CIA man was stunned. During all the months he had worked for Marshall, this was the first time the colonel had offered him a drink.

"Here's to A-410," the colonel said, raising his glass. "I knew I could count on Reese."

Clifford slowly sipped at the brandy. He was more of a bourbon on the rocks man himself, but it was the thought that counted.

"Has that armor support I requested shown up at the camp yet?" Marshall asked.

"Yes, sir. They closed in this afternoon."

"Good," Marshall said, taking another drink. "Good. Now all we need to do is sit back and wait."

Clifford drank in silence, but his mind was racing. Only a tanker would think that sending a couple of tanks up to a desolate hilltop fort was any kind of tactical stroke. The tanks' 90 mm guns could be a help if things got tough, but regardless of what Marshall thought, Clifford knew that tanks could be killed, too, particularly by the RPG rocket launchers the North Vietnamese carried.

"What about that woman?" Marshall broke into Clifford's thoughts. "That reporter, is she up there yet?"

"Yes, sir, Laura Winthrop. She arrived earlier this morning."

"Good." Marshall turned his glass in his hands. "That should keep her occupied for a while."

"What are you going to do when she gets back?"

Marshall smiled as he knocked off the last of his drink. "I told her I'd give her a chance to get a story. But I didn't say anything to her about getting it published. She can screw around up there all she wants, but when she gets back, I'm going to slap her ass right up against the wall."

"Why did you let her go up there then, sir?"

Marshall dropped his smile. "I did it to buy time while I had her investigated and worked up a cover story for the Dak Sang operation. I've already talked to her editor, and everything's taken care of. As soon as she gets back, she either keeps her stupid mouth shut or she flies out on the next plane."

18

July 3, Dak Sang

When Reese got back to Laura, it was almost time for dinner. Now that the mess hall was in full operation Reese had more to offer her than a can of cold Cs. In fact, in celebration of the day's successful mission the Nung cook had gone out of his way to prepare a special meal. A resupply flight had brought in enough chickens and a small pig for a traditional Nung feast.

"Sorry to have been so long," he said, sitting down across the table from the reporter. "But I think I can make it up to you. We're having a feast tonight to celebrate opening the camp, and I think you'll enjoy it."

Laura sniffed the air. "I've been smelling something good for the past hour, and I love Chinese food."

"This is more than just Chinese food," Santelli said. "Our cooks could open up a restaurant and get rich if they weren't working for us."

Laura sat at the head table with Reese, his A-team members, Dublin's tankers, the engineers and the strike force officers. The Nung troops would eat in shifts so that they could keep the perimeter manned until dark. They had kicked an NVA company to hell today, but that didn't mean there weren't more of them out there.

With little fanfare the Nungs brought out the first course: barbecued pork served with savory vegetables and rice, and everyone dug in for a traditional Nung feast. The only thing that wasn't traditional about the meal was that the Nungs weren't offering toasts between every course. Reese had flown in several cases of beer, but he was rationing it to two cans a man, and that wasn't enough for a Nung drinking bout. He was trying to give his people an evening off, but there was no guarantee that the NVA would honor the holiday. As soon as the sun was down, everyone would have to be back in their holes, ready to go to work at a moment's notice.

Laura was talking to Ian Dublin, and the Boston Irish tanker was giving her his opinion on how the war was being run. Like most Irishmen, Dublin had a lyrical lilt to his voice and a way with words. Laura laughed at something the tanker said and then shot a quick glance over to Reese to see if he was watching her.

"By the way, Captain," Santelli said out of the corner of his mouth, "I'll be out in the perimeter all night, so you'll have the bunker to yourself."

"You don't have to do that," Reese said. "I won't be needing it."

Santelli looked down the table at Laura. "That's not what it looks like to my practiced eye. If that lady isn't hot after your body, then I'm not Italian."

Reese grinned broadly. "Thanks, Jack."

"*Non chi vulo niente,* as they say back home."

"What the hell does that mean?"

"Loosely translated it means, 'be my guest.'"

Reese laughed and clapped him on the shoulder. "I'll return the favor first chance I get."

"I'll hold you to that promise, sir." Santelli grinned. "Maybe I'll get lucky, too, one of these days and talk a certain nurse I know into coming up here for a visit."

Shortly after the remains of the last course were cleared away, Reese glanced at his watch. "Gentlemen," he announced, "the sun's down and it's about time we got ready for our evening's activities."

As the Green Berets left to go to their night duty stations and Dublin's tankers returned to their iron chariots, Laura rejoined Reese. "What happens now?" she asked, looking up at him.

He smiled tightly. "Now we get down in our holes and wait for the sun to come up again."

"That sounds simple enough."

"That depends on the dinks," Reese said. "Right now we're still mostly reacting to their moves rather than really calling the shots around here ourselves. Give me a couple of more weeks, though, and we should be a little more on top of things."

"But, according to what Jack said, you totally destroyed a North Vietnamese company today. Won't that keep things quiet for a while?"

Reese frowned. "I sure as hell hope it does. But I don't have a good feel for how many more NVA units might be hiding in the woods around here. We still might be facing more than we can handle, and we can't take any chances until we know this AO a little better."

"So what do you do at night while you're waiting for the NVA to show up?" she asked. "You don't stay in a bunker all night, do you?"

He shook his head. "No. I check the perimeter to make sure everything's squared away, talk to the guys who're pulling the radio watch and then I try to get a couple of hours of sleep."

Laura cocked her head and looked at him. "Where do you sleep?"

Reese looked surprised. "Over there," he said, pointing to a small sandbagged bunker close to the CP.

She smiled slyly. "I've never seen the Special Forces version of a man's bedroom before."

The unspoken invitation in her voice caused a chill to run down Reese's back. This was the most unique proposition he had ever had, but he wasn't about to let that stand in his way. "I'll be glad to give you a guided tour."

She reached out and touched his arm. "I'd really like that, Mike."

Reese downed the last of his beer and got to his feet. "Let's go."

Reese felt more than a little self-conscious as he walked to his bunker with Laura at his side. Even though it was dark he felt that every man's eye was following them every inch of the way, each man wishing he were taking her tonight, but he wished it didn't have to be under these circumstances. He knew, though, that he was lucky even to have this chance. Now that his company was Hatchet Force he didn't think he'd be getting back to Saigon anytime in the near future.

"Duck your head," he warned, turning the flashlight toward the low beam over the door.

Once inside Reese shone the flashlight beam against the back wall to illuminate the small bunker as he made his way over to his bunk against the wall.

"This is nice and homey," she said, sitting down on the cot. "It kind of reminds me of summer camp."

Reese laughed. "You spent summer camp sleeping in a bunker?"

"No." She patted the poncho liner blanket beside her. "The cots and the sleeping bags."

"I really shouldn't be doing this," he said as he sat beside her.

"Why not?"

"Well, for one thing, I need to be ready if anything happens tonight."

"Keep your boots on." She grinned. "That actually might be fun."

"Also—" he grinned back "—we share all our goodies out here in the field, and I don't think there's enough of you to go around."

"I don't know about that," she said. "Maybe after you're done I can call that nice Lieutenant Santelli in and then maybe your radio operator. What's his name, Torres?"

"Anything for a story, right?"

"You got that shit right, Reese," she said with a laugh. "The story always comes first."

"And I'm part of the story?" he asked. "Just who are you writing for—*Playboy?*"

"Actually, that's not a bad idea. I could do a piece called 'Love in the Bunkers.'"

Reese laughed. "I'm sure Hugh Hefner would love that story, particularly if I did a photo layout of you to go with the article."

She smiled, leaned back against the wall and folded her hands behind her head, her full breasts stretching the fabric of her shirt. "You'd like that, wouldn't you?"

"I've always wanted to be a *Playboy* photographer," he admitted.

"Wouldn't every man?"

Unlike the night he had spent with Laura at her villa, Reese felt awkward with her tonight. Maybe it was just because every man in the camp knew he was in the bunker with her, or maybe it was caused by the reason for her presence in Dak Sang. Whatever the reason, he felt like a high school boy in the back seat of a parked car for the first time.

Laura sensed his hesitation. She unbuttoned the top of her safari shirt and let it hang open to expose her breasts. In the dim light of the flashlight Reese could see the shadowed roundness of her full breasts. He swallowed hard but couldn't take his eyes away.

"It's too bad you didn't think to stock the bar before I came," she said softly, fully aware of the effect she was having on him. "I could sure use a drink or two right about now."

"Actually, you're in luck," Reese said, snapping his eyes away and reaching for his rucksack, which was leaning against the wall at the foot of his bunk. "I just happen to have a bottle of brandy in here."

"Good," she purred. "I like brandy."

"I don't have any glasses, so we'll have to rough it."

That brought a soft laugh to Laura's lips. "Rough it? Drinking brandy out of a bottle is your idea of roughing it? You have me trapped out here in your jungle lair, miles from civilization, where everyone watches me piss into a hole in the ground, and you have the balls to apologize for offering me a drink out of a bottle?"

Reese shrugged. "I just don't want you to think that we Special Forces people are uncouth."

"Uncouth?" she repeated, shaking her head as she reached for the bottle. "Jesus, Reese, I'd never accuse you of anything as civilized as that." She took a long drink and handed the bottle back to him. "That's good."

He took a long pull from the bottle, savoring the brandy in his mouth before swallowing it. The rich taste of the liquor went well with the faint scent of her perfume. He reached out and finished unbuttoning her shirt so that he could smell her perfume better.

She shrugged out of her shirt and reached for the zipper of her jeans. In a second they were at her feet, and she was naked. The dim lights threw deep shadows over the lush curves of her body. The valley between her breasts and the patch of blond hair at the juncture of her thighs were in darkness, but he felt them drawing him closer. Bending down, he started unlacing his boots.

"I thought you said you needed to keep your boots on," she said softly as she lay back on the bunk.

"I can make an exception this time," he said, hurriedly shrugging off his fatigues. "Anything so you can get your story."

She laughed and pulled him down on top of her. When she felt his ready hardness, she opened her legs wider, and he moved between them. Raising her knees, she reached down and guided him inside her.

He sank into her inner softness and paused for a moment to savor the feeling again. But the urgency of the moment was too strong. He started thrusting into her, moving slowly at first, but then riding her faster and faster as the sensations built. Much too soon he felt his climax start. Unable to hold it back, he collapsed on top of her, shuddering and shaking as he gave in to it.

She held him in her arms and stroked the back of his neck as he struggled to catch his breath. "Mike?"

He nuzzled her neck. "Yes?"

"Are you still mad at me?"

He chuckled softly. "That's a hell of a thing to ask a guy at a time like this."

"Well, are you?" she asked in a small voice.

He slid his face down to her breasts. "Do I act like I'm mad at you?"

"No," she said. "But . . ."

She sucked her breath in when his mouth fastened on her nipple. Her legs opened, and he positioned himself between them again. He was aware that she hadn't had an orgasm and, since he was in no danger of going off again for quite some time, he could take care of her now.

This time their lovemaking went more slowly, and he was able to soak up fully the sensations of making love to this beautiful woman. The hot, slick tightness of being inside her, the play of sleek muscles under the smooth skin of her thighs and the deep softness of her breasts pressed against his chest spurred him on to thrust himself even deeper into her.

Her legs came up around his hips to lock him into her as he rode her faster and faster. Her fingers dug into his shoulders, her breath came in short gasps, and she arched her back to press her breasts even tighter against the hard muscles of his chest.

A gasping cry escaped her lips and, when he felt her inner muscles clamp tightly against him, he couldn't resist the pressure any longer. He raised himself, his back arched, and gave himself over completely to the pleasure washing over him.

When it was over, Reese lay beside her, his head cradled on her breast and breathed in the scent of her body—a subtle mixture of perfume, fresh sweat and sex. It was the most powerful scent he had ever smelled, and he felt it lighting a fire in his mind. Jesus! A man could get used to having this woman around on a permanent basis.

The idea shocked him. It had been a long time since he had even thought of trying to start another full-time relationship. He still wasn't divorced from Judy yet, and here he was feeling like a schoolboy falling in love for the first time.

After spending his first night with Laura in her Saigon apartment, he had wanted to try for a rematch as soon as he could manage it. But he had given no thought to trying to claim her for his own; it just hadn't crossed his mind. Now, though, he didn't know what to think.

Even though she had come to him freely tonight, she had done nothing to indicate that she considered him anything other than a good lay. So, until he had a better idea where he stood with her, he had to get himself under control before he made a complete ass of himself.

For the time being, though, simply being a good lay was enough for him.

19

July 4, Dak Sang

When Laura dropped off to sleep, Reese carefully disengaged himself and stood. He would have loved to spend the rest of the night sleeping beside her, but he knew better than that. Quickly he got back into his fatigues and, leaving the flashlight on in case she woke up and was disoriented, slipped out of the bunker.

It was a little before midnight, and a soft rain was falling when he headed over to check in with the night duty NCO in the command bunker. He welcomed the rain and didn't even try to cover up. A little rain would do a lot to settle the construction dust and make Dak Sang more livable for the next couple of days.

On the bad side, though, too much rain would turn the place into a quagmire. Rain also meant clouds, and since the hill was in the middle of a valley, the clouds would hang between the hills longer than they would on the plains. That would cut them off from air support if they needed it. He would have to check the weather report for the next couple of days and see what was in store.

Sergeant Pierce was on radio watch in the bunker, and he looked up when Reese walked in. "You're up late, sir."

"Couldn't sleep," he said with a straight face as he walked over to the coffeepot and poured himself a cup. "What's hot tonight?"

"Nothing." Pierce shook his head. "Everything's quiet. The LT's down on the perimeter, and the tankers are keeping one man awake while the rest sleep in their cans, so we're pretty well covered."

"I've got to remember to ask the engineers to build us a tower before they leave," Reese said. "We need to get a searchlight up there and maybe one of those ground surveillance radar sets."

"It wouldn't hurt," Pierce agreed. "And we could put one set of our antennae up there, too."

"What's the weather report for the next couple of days?"

Pierce flipped through a stack of papers on a clipboard. "It looks like the summer's going to be late again. The monsoon's moving back in for at least the next couple of days." In the Central Highlands there was usually a break in the rain in July, but it looked as though it was going to be delayed for a week or so.

Reese drained the last of his coffee. "I'm going to bunk down here for a couple of hours, and then I'll relieve Jack out in the perimeter."

"Torres will be taking over at two o'clock," Pierce said. "And I'll tell him you're here."

SHORTLY AFTER 0100 hours three NVA sappers dressed in black pajamas and head scarves crept forward on their bellies toward the three machine-gun bunkers on the east side of the hill. They had made their way successfully through the outer ring of concertina and were working on the second ring of wire.

Each sapper carried a pair of ten-pound high-explosive satchel charges. The first charge had to blow gaps in the inner wire so the infantry could storm through, and the second was to be thrown through the front apertures of the bunkers to take out the guns. The sappers' only other weapon was a Tokarev pistol stuck in the waistband of their pants. If even one of them survived their suicide mission, it would be a miracle.

A hundred yards behind the sappers two assault platoons of North Vietnamese infantry lay waiting in the shadows at the bottom of the hill. Along with their usual weapons and grenades, they also carried assault ladders and straw mats to throw on top of the barbed wire barriers so that they could scramble up over the obstacles.

Two hundred yards beyond them, back in the tree line, two more NVA platoons with RPG launchers and machine gunners were poised to give supporting fire and to reinforce the assault group if they got hung up. Farther on in the jungle an NVA mortar team stood ready with three 82 mm mortars. The tubes had been sighted in earlier that afternoon, and the stack of six-and-a-half-pound HE projectiles had all their propellent charges cut for the correct range. The NVA were determined to get revenge on A-410 for the destruction of their comrades in Cambodia. The first satchel charge explosion would be the signal for the attack to begin.

The North Vietnamese sappers were good. On their way up the gentle hillside they had found and deactivated several of the trip flares and claymores in the outer and middle ring of wire. They had just cleared the tanglefoot and were entering the inner ring of concertina when Santelli started his inspection of the perimeter.

The sapper in front of the machine-gun bunker in the Second Platoon sector froze in place when he heard the American officer talking quietly to the men in the bunker not twenty feet away from him.

The young North Vietnamese soldier had once been a university student, and he spoke English very well. He started listening to the low voices, thinking that he could pick up some useful information. After a moment curiosity overcame his caution and he started crawling forward again.

He was so intent on trying to hear what was being said that he let his attention wander. The bulky satchel charge in his hand brushed against a thin, dark wire set close to the ground. The wire was attached to a mouse trip trigger for a booby-trapped claymore. It was a light touch, but it was enough to do the job.

The blinding flash of the exploding claymore lit up the darkened perimeter.

The mine had been set to fire at a forty-five-degree angle to the wire, and the sapper was only a few feet away when it detonated. Most of the seven hundred .25-caliber steel balls in the mine tore through his body. The blast also detonated the satchel charges he was carrying. The sapper was dead before he even had a chance to know he had done something wrong.

Grabbing the claymore clackers in both hands, the Nung rifleman in the bunker slammed down on the firing handles of the detonators once, twice, three times. Two more claymore explosions blasted steel balls across their front and another of the sappers died.

At the base of the hill NVA signal whistles shrilled in the darkness. The two assault platoons leaped to their feet and raced for the wire, firing their AK-47s from the hip. The Nung machine gunner in the bunker brought his M-60 into play, rapping out quick, short bursts through the firing aperture when he saw their shadowy figures.

Santelli grabbed the land-line phone in the bunker and started cranking on the handle as the men around the perimeter opened up. Lines of red tracer fire shot into the dark and were answered by green return fire.

"Torres!" the lieutenant shouted when the phone was picked up at the other end. "We're being hit! Give me some light!"

RIGHT AFTER the second claymore went off, the tanker standing guard in the command hatch of the turret of Asskicker, the platoon's One One command tank, snapped on the seventy-five-candlepower xenon searchlight mounted on top of the main gun. Using the commander's override controls in the cupola, he swung the turret around to bring the searchlight to bear on the north side of the perimeter.

The blinding beam of light illuminated dark, screaming figures racing for the wire. The tanker pulled back twice on the charging handle for the .50-

caliber machine gun mounted on top of the cupola and pressed his thumbs down on the big gun's trigger. Ma Deuce began to speak.

In the tree line the RPG gunners of the fire support element saw the steady stream of fire from the .50, took aim at the searchlight and fired. Almost simultaneously three 85 mm rocket-propelled antitank grenades left their launchers. A few yards out of the muzzles the secondary propellent charges ignited and sped the deadly antitank rounds on to their target.

The first RPG-7 rocket missed completely, but the second round slammed into the base of the tank searchlight and detonated. The white-hot jet of explosive gases from the shaped charge warhead cut through the xenon light housing and blasted it to pieces.

The third RPG antitank hit low on the cupola. Deflected upward by the sloping armor, the blast shattered the upper body of the tanker and silenced his weapon.

The other tankers had already scrambled into their vehicles, cranked up the tanks' engines, battened down the hatches and were ready to fight. Sliding into the command hatch of One Two, Dublin cursed the fact that he didn't have a searchlight mounted on his tank. He would be unable to fire accurately until some illumination was dropped on the perimeter.

He punched the radio switch. "Asskicker," he called to the One One tank, "this is Assassin. What's your status, over?"

All he heard was squelch over his headphones, as if someone was keying a mike but not speaking. "Asskicker, this is Assassin. What the fuck's wrong with you people over there? Let me talk to Miles."

"Assassin," came a scared young voice. "This is Asskicker. Ralph's dead, and the sergeant can't get his body out of the hatch."

Dublin recognized the voice of One One's gunner, a new kid who hadn't been in a firefight yet. "This is Assassin," the tank commander answered calmly. "You just hang in there, son. Get your main gun loaded with canister and stand by. And get Sergeant Miles on the horn as soon as you can."

"Yes, sir."

Dublin shook his head ruefully. This was just what he needed—a scared shitless, FNG tank gunner in the middle of the camp being overrun. He tripped the intercom switch. "Gunner, as soon as you can get a target, fire."

LAURA WAS STARTLED AWAKE when the first claymore went off. For a moment she was disoriented and didn't know where she was. Then the second charge detonated, shocking her into complete awareness. The camp was under attack!

Her heart racing, she scrambled into her clothes as fast as she could and ran to the door of the bunker. Peering around the corner, she saw tracer fire coming from the bunkers on the perimeter. Then, from the corner of her eye, she saw the RPGs hit the tank. It looked as if the tank exploded, and she saw the outline of the guard silhouetted against the blast.

For a second she froze, hugging the sandbag wall of the bunker. The only thought that came to her mind was that she had to get to the command bunker. Reese and his men would be there, and they would know what she should do. Doubling over the way she had seen men do in war movies, she dashed out into the open and ran across the open ground for the bunker.

SERGEANT BOB ROHM was racing for his battle station at the camp's mortar pits when the NVA opened up with the mortar barrage. Dropping the rounds down the tubes as fast as they could, the enemy gunners had four HE rounds in the air before the first one even hit.

The first round landed several yards to his right. Ducking too late to avoid the shrapnel, Rohm continued for the mortar pits in front of him. The second round landed directly on the corner of the ammunition storage bunker next to the gun pits. The resulting blast swept him off his feet, slamming him to the ground. The third round exploded directly at the base of one of the camp's mortars, adding fragments from the tube to the shrapnel flying through the air.

Ears ringing from the blast, Rohm staggered to his feet and ran the last few yards to the mortar pits. He saw that the one tube had been destroyed, and he ran on to the second pit. It was tipped over, and he didn't waste time checking if it was still safe to fire. The third 81 mm tube was undamaged, and snatching an illumination round from the ready racks, he dropped it into the tube.

The illumination flare popped over the base of the hill, and Rohm frantically cranked on the elevation wheel, trying to bring the tube up to maximum elevation. He had to get the light over the camp. He dropped another round, and it burst into life over the edge of the perimeter.

By the time he fired the third illumination round, three of the Nung mortar crew finally arrived. Two of them ran to set up the other tube while the third started dropping illumination rounds as fast as he could.

Leaving the Nungs to their work, Rohm vaulted over the sandbag parapet and ran for the 106 mm recoilless rifle pit fifty yards away. If he could get it into the action, maybe he could turn the NVA back.

Santelli was trying to call in the prearranged artillery fire concentrations when the land-line phone to the command bunker went dead. Snatching up his M-16, he ran out of the bunker just in time to see the first mortar rounds impact on the camp. He dived for cover, his arms over his head.

He was getting to his feet when he saw movement out of the corner of his eye. He spun around, his M-16 already leveled, when he recognized the figure. "Laura!" he shouted as the second volley of NVA mortar shells started falling. "Get down!"

20

July 4, Dak Sang

Sergeant Torres had gone to the command bunker early to take over the radio watch. He and Pierce had been going over the evening's radio logs when the first claymore detonated. Shoving Pierce away from the radios, Torres snatched up the handset, switched the AN/GRC-49 radio over to the artillery frequency and keyed the mike. "Red Leg Five Niner, Red Leg Five Niner, this is Bent Talon, over."

Reese awoke with the first explosion. He leaped from his bunk, and dashed into the radio room. "Where are they?" he asked Pierce.

"They're hitting the northern sector," the team sergeant replied. "I was on the phone with the LT, but he was cut off."

"Is he okay?"

"I don't know."

Just then Silk Wilson, dressed only in his fatigue pants, came racing down the steps to get his aid bag. Since the dispensary hadn't been completed yet, Wilson had stored the team's medical supplies in the command bunker. Snatching the bag from the pile of medical gear, he quickly donned a flak jacket, grabbed an M-16 and bounded back up the stairs. Men were being wounded and killed in the camp, and his job was to be out there with them.

IN THE NEXT INTERVAL between the mortar volleys Santelli picked himself off the ground and ran over to where Laura lay curled up.

"You okay?" he asked, crouching beside her. Not giving her time to answer, Santelli scooped her up off the ground and, cradling her in his arms like a child, sprinted the last few yards to the steps leading down into the command bunker.

Reese looked up as Laura raced down the stairs, followed by Santelli. "You okay?"

When she nodded, he turned to Santelli. "What's the situation?"

"It's a major assault," the lieutenant answered. "We've got to get the artillery—"

A brace of mortar shells hit the end of the bunker, cutting Santelli off abruptly. Laura choked off a scream as the blast shook the structure and dust rained down from the roof. "The antennae are down!" Torres shouted from the radio console. "I got cut off! I can't get through to the artillery!"

Reese snatched up one of the backpack Prick-77 radios and raced for the steps leading out of the bunker. Torres grabbed his M-16 and ran after his commander.

DUBLIN PEERED through the vision blocks in his cupola, trying to pick a target. With all the fire out there he had buttoned the hatch, and the night view through the vision blocks was marginal. Even with the flickering artillery illumination it was difficult to find good targets for his tank's weapons.

The attack was coming from his left front, and he had spun the turret around to face it, but he couldn't see well enough to pick out a clear target. If Ass-kicker had still had her xenon searchlight going, he could have fired the main guns. But as it was, he was afraid he would hit the friendly bunkers if he tried to use the 90s.

He could, however, try the cupola-mounted .50 caliber. Making sure he wasn't shooting into the back of a bunker, he thumbed the trigger, marching the tracers into the wire.

OUTSIDE, Reese and Torres had finally found a sheltered spot in a shell hole to try to call for help. Slipping the radio off his back, Reese set it to the firebase frequency while Torres erected the long whip antenna and screwed it into the radio's antenna socket.

"Red Leg Five Niner, Red Leg Five Niner," Reese shouted into the handset, "this is Bent Talon Six. Fire concentrations Alpha, Charlie and Delta. Give me illumination on Bravo. How copy, over?"

"Bent Talon Six," came the calm voice from the artillery fire direction center miles away. "This is Red Leg Five Niner. Roger, fire HE on Alpha, Charlie and Delta. Illumination on Bravo. Wait one. Out."

"This is Talon Six. Get it coming, goddamn it! We got dinks in the fucking wire!"

"Roger Talon Six. Keep your pants on, man. It's coming as fast as it can. Out."

Reese hugged the ground, cursing the calm voice of Red Leg Five Niner back at the artillery fire direction center. Not for the first time he hated all the cannon cockers back at their nice secure little firebases. Five Niner wouldn't be so damned calm if he were getting overrun by screaming NVA troops.

"Bent Talon Six, this is Red Leg Five Niner. Shot over. Illumination on the way."

"Where's my fucking HE!" Reese yelled.

"This is Red Leg Five Niner. The HE's coming up. Out."

The first of the 155 mm howitzer illumination rounds burst over the patrol base with a faint pop. The flickering yellow-white flare descending on its parachute illuminated a scene straight out of hell.

Dark figures, their AKs blazing green tracers, scrambled over the ladders and mats thrown on top of the rolls of concertina wire. Claymores exploded with bright flashes, and the dark figures screamed when the steel balls ripped through their ranks, but more of their comrades took their place.

Chicom grenades arced through the air in return and exploded against the bunkers with dull thumps. Steady streams of red M-60 tracer fire blazed from the machine-gun bunkers. The Thumper gunners fired their 40 mm grenades point-blank into the faces of the NVA.

Just as the first artillery flare flickered out and died, two more popped into life above the camp, and the hellish scene came to life again. Now the artillery HE rounds were falling, but they were falling at the base of the hill and the tree line, too far away to do any good.

THE ONLY HEAVY WEAPONS in the camp that could bear on the attackers were the single 81 mm tube still in action and the 106 mm recoilless rifle. Rohm made it through the mortar barrage to the 106 pit without getting hit. Two of the Nungs were already there, but they were huddled against the base of the sandbags to keep out of the rain of shrapnel. When they saw Rohm, they hurried to get the gun ready to fire.

As the Nung loader slid a round into the breech and slammed it shut, Rohm peered through the gunsight and pushed the firing button. The backblast lit up the gun pit as the 106 roared and flame belched from the muzzle.

The round the Nungs had loaded was a HEP round. It burst in the middle of the wire, blowing a new hole for the NVA to swarm through. "Fléchette!" Rohm yelled, laying the gun on another target. "Goddamn it, give me fléchette!"

As the Nungs scrambled in the ammo bunker to find one of the deadly antipersonnel rounds, the NVA mortar crews traversed their tubes to bring them to bear on Rohm and the 106. They had seen the backblast of the recoilless rifle and knew the threat it presented to their infantry. Dropping their rounds down the tubes as fast as they could, they walked their fire into the gun pit.

The first 82 mortar round landed outside the gun pit, but the shrapnel caught one of the Nung loaders full in the chest, killing him instantly. The second round hit the top of the sandbag parapet, and the third landed near the muzzle of the gun. The blast threw Rohm out of the gun pit, and he lay motionless on the ground.

REESE SAW Rohm's gun pit take the first hit and then several more as the NVA mortars found the range. There would be no help from him now. The tankers were firing their .50s, but even the steady stream of fire from the heavy machine guns wasn't slowing the enemy down. There were just too many of them.

The NVA support element had moved up closer to the perimeter to get out of the rain of friendly artillery fire. Their exploding RPG rounds added to the carnage as they fired their rocket launchers almost point-blank at the bunkers. One bunker in the First Platoon squad sector took an RPG round through the aperture and exploded with a bone-shaking crump. The bunker's machine gun fell silent.

Suddenly the assault platoons were through the wire and swarming over the silent bunker. When Reese saw the dark figures of the NVA racing through the camp firing their AKs from the hip, he realized it was time to fire the Firecracker mission, the final defensive fires that Torres had prearranged on the day they had moved into Dak Sang.

Every time the team moved to a new location one of the first things they did was to register an NVA-in-the-wire artillery shoot with their supporting artillery battery. This was a desperate last-ditch measure, as dangerous to the defenders as it was to the attackers, and the situation was rarely bad enough that they had to use it. But this was clearly one of those times. If he didn't shoot it, they were all going to be killed, anyway. "Shoot the Firecracker mission," he told Torres.

"Red Leg Five Niner, this is Bent Talon," Torres radioed. "Request Firecracker on my location. How copy, over?"

The FDC paused. He was reluctant to fire the Firecracker mission on top of the camp, and with good reason. The 155 mm Firecracker artillery rounds were thin-walled shells loaded with small bomblets similar to the Air Force's cluster bombs. When the artillery shells burst in the air over the target, the bomblets were released to rain down onto the ground. Each bomblet was just slightly larger than a golf ball and contained an explosive charge with a thick wire coil wrapped around it. When it hit the ground and detonated, the fragments of the wire could kill to a range of about five yards and could wind up fifteen yards away.

Since each shell carried dozens of bomblets and dispersed them over an area the size of a football field, it was like being caught outside in a rainstorm. You could run, but you'd still get wet. Anyone caught out in the open when the Firecrackers popped was going to be hit.

"Bent Talon Six, this is Five Niner," the FDC finally answered. This time the voice was tense. Lives were on the line, American lives. "Give authority for a Firecracker mission on those coordinates, over."

Reese snatched the radio handset from Torres. "This is Bent Talon Six, Captain Michael Reese, the camp commander," he shouted. "I'm authorizing this fire mission. Shoot it, goddamn it! Shoot it!"

"This is Five Niner. Roger, sir. On the way. Good Luck. Out."

Reese took a deep breath. "Take Cover!" he shouted as loud as he could. "Firecracker! Take cover!"

Over the roar of small-arms fire Reese heard the speeding freight train sound of the incoming artillery rounds. He and Torres curled up into little balls in the bottom of their hole and put their hands over their heads.

The world exploded around them.

It sounded like a Tet celebration in Saigon, except that the pops of these Firecrackers were louder. Each pop meant that hundreds of deadly razor-sharp shards of steel were whizzing through the air. When they met flesh, they struck deep.

Most of the flesh they met was North Vietnamese. One had a bomblet explode when it hit him and his head vanished in a red haze. Most of the rest died from dozens of small wounds that bled them to death in mere seconds.

In some cases, though, the flesh was American or Nung. A Nung in First Platoon died. He had been deafened by a grenade explosion and hadn't heard the call to get under cover. He had been already wounded, but he would have lived had the Firecracker round not finished him off.

The engineers were all huddled under their bull-dozer, but one man had his leg sticking out. He took a half a dozen wounds in the lower leg with one shot.

Others took single hits as some of the small frags found their way into the bunkers. The North Vietnamese, however, died by the dozens.

21

July 4, Dak Sang

When the last of the six Firecracker rounds detonated, a strange silence fell over the camp, a lull in the firestorm. All that could be heard were the screams and moans of the wounded and the dying.

Slowly, one by one, the Nungs came out of their holes and bunkers and opened up again on the surviving North Vietnamese in the wire. It was a slaughter.

Slightly wounded NVA, stunned by the sudden fury of the artillery attack, were gunned down where they stood. Bodies hanging in the wire were shot again and again until they were torn apart. One badly wounded NVA lying out of the direct line of fire screamed his pain over and over again. It took three Thumper grenades to silence him.

The few surviving members of the assault platoons frantically tried to retreat, unmindful of the cuts as the razor-sharp points on the concertina opened even more wounds in their bodies. Deadly fire from the bunkers thumped into their backs, and many of them stayed where they were, hanging lifelessly on the wire.

Torres kept the artillery illumination going while he chased the NVA back into the woods with HE. Even Dublin's tanks got in a few main gun rounds now that the NVA were streaming back down the hill and they had a clear shot at them.

Above the sound of firingz, the voices of the Nung wounded could be heard crying out for the medics. The NVA were in full retreat, but the victory hadn't been without a heavy cost. The medics, both the A-team's and the engineers', scrambled around inside the camp, locating and treating the casualties.

Of the Americans only Rohm had been seriously hurt. He had taken several chunks of mortar shrapnel that had opened his chest and abdomen. Wilson did what he could, plugging a bag of blood expander into his arm and preparing him for immediate evacuation.

As soon as the firing died down, Reese and Torres put in a call to Kontoum to request a priority Dust-off for the more seriously wounded. Several of the men, including Rohm, wouldn't last until dawn.

LAURA SAT UNNOTICED at the small table against the wall of the bunker. Someone had handed her a cup of coffee to calm her nerves, but it had grown cold in her hands as the battle had raged outside. She was beginning to believe that the Special Forces' answer to any crisis was to have a cup of coffee. Now that she was safe, as safe as she could be anywhere at Dak Sang, she took stock of her surroundings. The A-team's medics had brought casualties into the bunker, turning it into an aid station for some of the less seriously wounded who wouldn't be Medevaced.

The wounded Nungs were stoic, almost cheerful in their bloodied bandages. They chattered in their dialect and passed cigarettes back and forth with smiles on their faces. Laura had no way of knowing that the smiles were the Nungs' response to pain, their way of denying its existence.

Rather than just sit there and feel useless, she got up to see if there was anything she could do to help the medics. She had no medical training, but there had to be something she could do, even if it was merely to hand out cigarettes and cups of water.

Almost apologetically she approached the Nung medic. "Is there something I can do to help you?"

The medic looked up at her in surprise. "Please, missy," he said. "They *beaucoup* thirsty—" he nodded toward the row of men he had already bandaged "—need water."

Dumping the cold coffee from her cup, she filled it from the water cooler by the coffeepot and approached the first man, a young Nung with both of his hands and forearms bandaged almost to the elbow. Laura knew he had to be at least eighteen to serve in the Mike Force, but he was so slight that he looked as though he couldn't have been over fourteen. He, too, had a smile on his face and a cigarette stuffed into the corner of his mouth.

"Do you want a drink?" she asked him. "Water?"

When the Nung nodded, she took the cigarette from his mouth and, holding his head, placed the cup to his lips.

The Nung drank deeply and pulled his head back from the cup. "*Cam on,* Missy Laura."

"How do you know my name?"

The young Nung's smile broadened. "You *co dep,* pretty woman. Come write about Nung camp. You *dai uy* girlfriend."

Laura felt her face flush, and she went back to the water cooler to refill the cup. The young Nung's eyes followed her, the smile still on his face.

For the rest of the night she went from one of the wounded to the next, helping them drink, lighting their cigarettes and talking to those who spoke English. Every man she helped smiled widely as if to deny his pain and not upset her. This was a side of the war she hadn't seen before, and it made her feel very insignificant.

OUTSIDE, the serious casualties had been moved out of the line of fire and were ready to be loaded onto the Dust-offs as soon as they appeared. Santelli worked with Wilson, coordinating the Medevac, while the team's other medic, Hayes, tended to the wounded. Rohm was awake and, though seriously wounded, Hayes thought he would survive if he got into surgery soon enough.

"Bent Talon, Bent Talon," came the voice over the radio handset. "This is Dust-off Three Five. I'm inbound to your location at this time. ETA two mikes. Stand by to illuminate the LZ, over."

"This is Talon Five," Santelli radioed back. "Roger. We have a strobe standing by. Approach from the east and you should be okay."

"Three Five, roger. I'm starting my descent now."

Santelli heard the faint sound of rotors in the distance. "Hit the strobe," he told Wilson.

The second the medic turned on the blue-white strobe the tree line erupted in fire. Green tracers streaked up to reach for the hovering ship, and the hollow, thunking sound of mortar firing could be heard. The Dust-off pilot pulled pitch instantly, hauling his ship safely out of the line of fire.

"Bent Talon, this is Dust-off Three Five," the pilot radioed down. "I can't set down with that fire coming in, over."

"Talon Five, roger," Santelli answered. "Just hang in there for a minute while I see if I can get our tanks to take those bastards out, over."

"Dust-off Three Five, wilco."

Santelli ran over to Dublin's tank, clambered onto the hull and pounded on the command hatch. Dublin popped his hatch and stuck his head out. "Can you take out a mortar for us so the Dust-offs can get in?"

"Does a fish have a watertight asshole?" the tanker replied. "Load HE!" he yelled down through the turret before turning back to Santelli. "Where are they?"

Crouching by the side of the tank's turret, Santelli scanned the jungle, looking for the spot where he had seen the telltale flashes of the mortar tubes. He pointed where the NVA fired again. "There's one."

"Got that little fucker," the tanker replied. Using the commander's sights, Dublin sighted in a little lower than the flash he'd seen. "Fire!"

The tank rocked back on its tracks as the main gun recoiled. The HE round burst in the tree line, lighting up the jungle for an instant.

"Raise it a bit and put it twenty yards to the right!" Santelli shouted.

Dublin made the correction and fired again. This time there was a bigger explosion as the tank gun round set off the mortar rounds the NVA had stacked by the tubes.

"Hit 'em again!"

The 90 roared once more, briefly lighting up the jungle.

"Thanks," Santelli said, patting the tanker on the shoulder.

"No sweat."

"Dust-off Three Five," Santelli radioed when he got back to the LZ. "This is Talon Five. How does it look now, over?"

"This is Three Five. It looks like you got him from up here. I'll try it again, over."

"Five, roger. Strobe on."

This time the chopper came in for a landing. The wounded were quickly loaded on board, and the Dust-off lifted off. As soon as it was clear, a second ship that had been standing by dropped down to take on its load of casualties. It took four flights to clear out all the wounded.

THE MORNING of the Fourth of July broke chilly and wet over Dak Sang. A solid bank of low clouds hung over the valley, and although it wasn't raining, a fine mist hung in the air, wetting everything like a heavy dew. Trapped by the clouds, a pall of smoke hung over the camp, adding to the limited visibility. The stench of battle was thick in the air, a gritty, oily mixture of cordite, explosives, blood and diesel thick enough to taste.

The dull light of dawn showed a scene of utter desolation. The mortar barrage had damaged or destroyed almost everything aboveground. The mess hall had caught fire and burned to the ground, the command bunker had been damaged, and the engineers' vehicles had taken hits. Only Dublin's tanks seemed to have come through unscathed, but even they had taken minor shrapnel damage.

Bodies littered the camp, both inside and outside the wire. The Nung dead had been gathered in one location during the night and covered with ponchos until they could be evacuated. But the enemy dead lay where they had fallen. There were more important things to do than to gather up their bodies. Later in the day the engineers would carve out a mass grave, and the corpses would be dumped in it before they became a sanitary hazard. But for now they lay where they had been killed.

The defenders' first task was to get to work rebuilding their defenses. Pierce had work parties patching up the barbed wire where holes had been cut or blown into the perimeter. Other work parties filled sandbags to rebuild damaged bunkers or lugged fresh ammunition supplies down to the fighting positions.

As soon as the work was started, Reese called for a quick team meeting in the command bunker. It was the first time they had all been together since the attack had started, and Reese was surprised to see how many of his men bore minor wounds, mostly from the Firecracker rounds. Hotchkiss, however, had taken an AK round through the upper arm but had refused evacuation, as had Baker who had taken a mortar shrapnel hit. No one had had any sleep, and they were filthy and bloodstained from moving casualties.

Laura was sleeping on a makeshift bed against the wall, and the men tried not to disturb her as they moved in on the coffee maker for a cup. Torres had kept the pot going all night long, and the strong, hot brew was welcomed.

"Okay," Reese said. "A few things before we get back to work. First off, the hospital says Rohm's going to make it. He'll probably be going home, but he should recover completely."

That was good news. The men of A-410 had been together a long time, and though they had taken their share of minor wounds, no one on the team had been killed since they had lost their old commander during the Tet Offensive.

Reese turned to Kowalski. "Ski, do you feel up to doing a little local recon this morning?"

Reese had tried to get an aerial recon mission to scout out the surrounding area at first light, but the solid cloud cover prevented the choppers from coming in. With the hills on either side of the valley holding the clouds in, it was too risky for the scout ships to attempt descent through the low ceiling. There was no point in adding dead chopper crews to the already too high friendly body count at Dak Sang.

The sergeant looked as battered and tired as any of them, but he wasn't wounded. "Exactly what did you have in mind, Captain?"

"I want you to take a couple of the Nungs and have a quick look around the tree line at the base of the hill. I need to know if they're still hanging around, but be careful out there and don't take any chances. If you see anything, get the hell out before you call it in.''

"You've got that shit right, sir," Kowalski answered wearily. "I've enjoyed just as much of this as I can stand for one twenty-four-hour period."

Reese laughed. "It all counts towards twenty, Sarge."

"Fuck that shit, sir," Kowalski muttered as he picked up his M-16 and headed up the steps.

"As for the rest of us," Reese continued, "while Ski's scouting around, we need to get back into business as fast as we can. CCC's got the resupply birds laid on, and they're bringing us ammo and a couple of 81s to replace the ones that got destroyed last night. They're also hauling more sandbags and wire. Get things squared away quickly, but keep your heads down while you're doing it. This might not be over yet."

HALF AN HOUR LATER Kowalski radioed Dublin from the tree line at the base of the hill, a note of hysteria rising in his voice. "Big Boy One Two, this is Bent Talon Alpha," he shouted. "Tanks! They've got fucking tanks down here!"

"One Three, roger," the tank commander answered calmly, a big grin spreading over his face. This was the moment every tanker with even half a pair of balls dreamed of—the chance to duke it out with enemy armor.

22

July 4, Dak Sang

The first time the North Vietnamese had committed tanks to combat had been in the battle at the Special Forces camp at Lang Vei back in February. In that contact there had been no American armor to hold off the attackers—ten Russian-made PT-76 light tanks. Despite a valiant fight by the SF defenders, who somehow managed to destroy seven of the PT-76s with hand-held M-72 LAW light antitank rockets, the NVA overwhelmed the camp with heavy loss of life.

Dublin vowed that this camp wasn't going to fall to enemy armor like Lang Vei. This time there were two made-in-America M-48A-3 Patton tanks defending the camp. The two Pattons were more than enough to hold off a horde of tin cans like the PT-76s.

The Russian-built PT-76 was a light amphibious tank originally designed to ford the rivers of Europe in the vanguard of invading Soviet mechanized armies. It was lightly armored but highly maneuverable, and the high-velocity 76 mm gun mounted in the turret was no lightweight weapon. Developed from the Panzer-killing Russian 76 mm high-velocity antitank gun of World War II, it packed a good punch with its shaped charge ammunition. Dublin's M-48s carried eleven inches of armored steel at the base of their turrets, but they were still vulnerable to the 76 mm gun.

If he wanted to come out on top of this armored duel, Dublin's only option was to make like a gunfighter from the Old West—beat the other guy to the draw, shoot fast and shoot to kill.

"Give me a location," Dublin quickly radioed back to Kowalski. "And then get the hell outta there and let us go to work."

The sound of the PT-76s moving in couldn't be heard over the sound of his own engine as his driver powered up. But when he peered through his sights, Dublin spotted movement in the northern edge of the woods. A patch of light olive-green paint showed against the deeper greens of the jungle.

"Gunner!" he shouted over the intercom as he grabbed the commander's override turret controls to bring the main gun to bear on the target. "HEAT! Dink cans! Range twelve hundred! Fire!"

On hearing the command "HEAT," the loader inside the turret basket reached to his right side for a 90 mm high-explosive antitank round, a shaped, armor-piercing shell. Drawing the heavy round out of the ready rack, he slammed it into the open breech of the main gun. The weight of the round tripped the feed tray, ramming the round into the gun, and the breechblock automatically locked behind it.

"Up!" the loader called out to let the gunner know the 90 was ready to fire.

Peering through his stereoscopic range-finding sights, the gunner searched for a clear shot at the enemy tanks. He could see little but foliage. Suddenly he spotted what he thought was a flash of olive-painted metal behind the trees. His finger squeezed the electrical firing trigger, and the 90 fired with a roar.

After loading the main gun, the loader had taken his position directly behind the weapon's breech, his back pressed tightly against the rear wall of the turret. When the gunner fired and the 90 recoiled, the breech would slam to the rear, the force of the propellent explosion being soaked up by the gun's hydraulic recoil springs.

When the springblock reached the limit of its recoil and ejected the empty cannon brass, it halted a bare hair's width in front of the loader's belt buckle. The buckle bore deep dents from the times when he hadn't hugged the back of the turret hard enough, but those were marks of pride for a tank gun loader. It took a pair of brass balls to stand behind the recoiling gun breech, and there were no lard-assed tank gun loaders.

Pivoting to the right in one smooth motion, the loader drew another HEAT round from the ready rack and slammed it into the feed tray. The feed tray rammed the round into the empty breech, the breech-block slammed up, locking into place, and the gun was loaded again. "Up!" he shouted.

In the command hatch Dublin spotted the strike of the first round through his sights. It had impacted to the right of a clump of bush in front of a massive tree. Using the commander's override, he traversed the gun to sight in on the tank himself. "Fire!"

This time the 90 mm HEAT round hit right at the junction of the PT-76's turret and hull.

The resulting explosion opened the light tank like a firecracker exploding in an empty tin can. The tank's turret, gun and all, went flying into the air, tumbling over and over before coming back to earth. A fireball of black smoke shot through with angry orange-red flame boiled up out of the jungle. No one got out of the wreckage.

One down! But how many more of those PT-76s were hiding out there? Dublin took control of the turret again, the electric motor whining as he traversed the gun, looking for another target.

From his left front a puff of smoke signaled that one of the enemy tanks had fired at him. The 76 mm round hit the rear of the turret, and Assassin rocked on her suspension with the blast. Dublin's face slammed into the sights, smashing his forehead against the rubber padding and opening a pressure cut over his right eye. "Is everybody okay?" he yelled.

When everyone checked in, he went back to his sights and swung the turret over to lock in on the second enemy tank. With the hatches buttoned down, the turret had quickly filled with the explosive gases from the main gun. Dublin's eyes stung from the harsh chemicals as well as the gash on his forehead, but he ignored the pain as he laid the gun on target. The main gun was ready with a HEAT round down the spout, and he fired as soon as the split image of the enemy tank in the stereoscopic sight reticle came together.

The second PT-76 didn't blow up like the first one. It just stopped dead in its tracks and the command hatch flew open. When the NVA TC scrambled out, Asskicker's gunner opened up, and the 7.62 mm co-ax gun cut him in two before he could clamber down from the hull.

"Hit him again!" Dublin shouted over the radio.

One One's gunner triggered his 90, and this time the PT-76 came apart.

A third enemy tank had been stationed behind the destroyed vehicle, and it fired through the smoke. The 76 mm HEAT round hit Asskicker at the turret ring right above the driver's position.

"We're hit!" Sergeant Miles screamed over the radio.

Dublin spun his cupola around and saw the driver's hatch blown open with the force of the explosion. "Get out!" he shouted.

The command hatch sprung open, and Miles slowly appeared, his right arm hanging limply at his side. He slid down over the side of the turret and staggered around behind the hull. Asskicker's gunner suddenly appeared under the rear of the tank and joined Miles. Apparently he had blown the emergency escape hatch on the belly of the tank and dropped out the bottom of the hull. The two men ran for cover as fast as they could.

The only man missing from the crew now was the loader. Dublin prayed that the kid was still alive, but he couldn't stop to worry. There was still another PT-76 out there trying to kill him.

Dublin's tank took another hit from the left, a glancing strike to the base of the turret. The fighting compartment rang with the blow, and the tank rocked back on its suspension, its tracks digging into the red earth.

The turret motor whined as Dublin sighted in on the PT-76 that had destroyed One One. "HEP!" he called down to the loader.

High-explosive plastic rounds were thin-walled shells containing C-4 plastic explosive and a base-detonating fuse. When the HEP round struck a target, the plastic explosive spread out over it like wet jelly before detonating.

Focusing in on the juncture of the turret and front hull of the enemy tank, he fired. The PT-76 moved backward with the force of the explosion, her front plates caving in. The second shot blew the turret off.

Dublin got a flash of the fourth PT-76's olive-green ass end through the foliage as it sped away down the jungle trail. Apparently the enemy tankers had had enough and didn't want to join their comrades. He fired at it, anyway, but the round impacted right behind the swiftly moving PT-76 as it disappeared into the jungle. There was no point in trying another shot.

The departure of the enemy tank didn't mean the battle was over. The report of the 90 had barely echoed away when the bunker line to Dublin's left erupted in small-arms fire.

Dublin swung the turret over and, following the lines of tracers, saw that the NVA infantry were massing again in the tree line at the base of the hill. Apparently this wasn't over yet, but now that he had daylight the NVA were going to find out what an M-48 could do against troops in the open.

"Canister!" he called out to the loader over the intercom.

Tripping the lever to open the main gun's breech, the loader unloaded the HEP round in the gun and put it aside. In its place he loaded an antipersonnel canister round, a shotgun shell for tank guns. Loaded with 1,280 steel balls, the canister round broke open a few yards from the muzzle and released them all in a giant shotgun blast.

Sighting in on the center of the target, Dublin triggered the 90. The roar of the main gun was immediately followed by the crack of the canister round blowing open as it released its deadly contents. The hundreds of steel pellets swept through the packed NVA ranks like a scythe.

In seconds he was reloaded and fired again. The gunner was firing the co-ax machine gun at the same time, covering the area while the main gun was being reloaded, keeping the enemy's heads down. Someone raised himself to launch an RPG, but the third canister round dissolved him and everyone in the vicinity into a bloody ruin.

By the third round of canister the surviving NVA broke and ran deeper into the jungle. Dublin kept pumping canister rounds down the hill until he could see no further sign of movement in the tree line. Finally the valley was quiet. He popped his hatch and climbed out of the tank. Now the battle was over.

THE RAIN HAD ENDED and the sun was shining weakly through a break in the clouds when Laura finally climbed out of the ruined command bunker. She was shocked to see what the battle had done to the camp. Before the attack Dak Sang had been a primitive outpost, but the camp had been neat and orderly in its fashion. Now it was a desolate, smoking ruin.

The air was filled with the bitter taste of gunpowder and explosives, overlaid with the sharp metallic tastes of fresh blood. The fires were out, but the smell of smoke still rose from the open driver's hatch of the destroyed tank. When the faint smell of overcooked meat reached her, she turned her head and gagged when she realized what the smell was—burned human flesh.

Laura turned back and slowly walked in the opposite direction. She wandered around the camp alone for almost an hour before Reese caught up with her. The Green Beret officer looked as though he were about to fall over and was moving in slow motion. In fact, everyone was totally exhausted, but there was work that had to be done before they could stop to clean up and rest.

"I've called for a chopper to take you out," he said. "I can't risk your staying here any longer."

"That's okay," she replied. "I don't want to be in your way anymore."

"You're not in my way," he said wearily, "but obviously this isn't the safest place in the world for you to be right now. I'd feel a lot better if you were back in Saigon."

Laura caught the tone of genuine concern for her in his voice. This was the first time he had voiced it without tying it in with the security concerns of his command. She knew that even though there was more she could cover here on her story, she needed to leave so she wouldn't be a further burden to him. He had enough problems without having to worry about her.

"I'll get my stuff ready."

He stepped up to her and put his hand on her shoulder. "It's best," he said gently. "This place is going to be a zoo here real soon when everyone flies in to see what happened last night. Plus, there's a real chance that the NVA aren't done with us yet."

"I understand."

Reese helped her gather her stuff and stayed with her, making small talk until the slick arrived. Neither one of them talked much about the battle, nor mentioned the few short hours they had spent together in Reese's bunker. The time wasn't right for talking about love, not when there was so much death all around them. That would come at a later time and in another place. Laura knew she would never see Dak Sang again.

When the slick arrived, Reese helped her into the back and buckled the seat belt over her lap. "I'll call you!" she yelled over the whine of the turbine.

This time, when the chopper circled above Dak Sang, climbing for altitude, Laura saw that Reese was looking up, watching her fly out of sight.

23

July 4, MACV-SOG Headquarters, Saigon

Dick Clifford stared out of the window of his second-story office in the MACV-SOG building. A cup of cold coffee sat unnoticed next to the report of the attack on the Hatchet Force camp at Dak Sang. Twelve of the Nungs were dead, another two dozen wounded, one of the SF sergeants had been seriously wounded, two more were nicked and the camp was in ruins. On top of that several of the engineers were wounded and one of Marshall's precious tanks had been blasted by RPGs, killing two of the crewmen and wounding a third.

Marshall had gotten his mini-Khe Sanh, all right, but at a tremendous cost to a valuable unit. A-410 wouldn't be back up to strength for well over a month, and the idea of using them as a Hatchet Force unit would have to be put on hold until then. All told it was a real monkey fuck. But he knew Marshall would be pleased. He had finally gotten to preside over a big battle, and now he could put himself in for a Legion of Merit for having thought up the bright idea of putting a single Mike Force company out in the woods all by themselves to draw enemy fire.

He would be disappointed, however, to hear that Laura Winthrop had somehow survived the battle.

Although he hadn't said it, Clifford knew the colonel had hoped that the reporter would be zipped into one of the body bags being flown out of Dak Sang today. It would have been the icing on his cake if she had died in the attack.

It was no news to the CIA man that his boss's interest in the war didn't go beyond what it would do to advance his career. Marshall often talked about the Pentagon desk job that was waiting for him in Washington when he got his first general's star at the end of his tour.

Clifford wasn't above thinking of his career first either, but there were limits to promoting one's self to the detriment of others, particularly when self-promotion resulted in casualties. There was little he could do after the fact, but maybe there was something he could do to prevent anything like this from happening again, at least to the men at A-410.

He rolled a sheet of paper into his typewriter. After typing his building number and Tan Son Nhut address in the top center of the page, he moved down two spaces and typed:

To: S-3, Command and Control Central
From: MACV-SOG Opns
Re: A-410

When he was done with the memo, he signed it, took a rubber stamp from his desktop and stamped FOUO on the top and bottom. Were he to classify the memo, it would have to be logged in and logged out, and Marshall went over the classified document logs.

But a memo "for official use only" didn't have to be accounted for. He put the memo in an envelope, wrote Snow's name on the front, stamped it FOUO and added an Eyes Only stamp. In the upper left-hand corner of the envelope he wrote the address of the SOG personnel staff section.

The memo would go out in the morning's courier flight to Kontoum, and Snow would have it in his hands by noon. Anyone along the way who handled the letter would think it was a routine administrative matter, and no one would take note of it, much less remember where it had originated.

REESE WAS COORDINATING with Pierce and Dublin to get a tank retriever up to take back the burned-out carcass of Asskicker when a Huey slick with a CCC call sign radioed that it was in-bound to Dak Sang.

With a final word to the tanker he and Pierce walked down to the chopper pad to meet whoever was coming. The unescorted slick touched down, and CCC's S-3, Major Snow, stepped to the ground. He quickly surveyed the destruction of the camp before walking over to Reese and Pierce.

"It looks like your people earned their pay last night," Snow commented dryly.

"Yes, sir," Reese answered. "They earned their pay and then some."

"Is there someplace we can talk?" the S-3 asked.

"We can go into what's left of the command bunker," Reese suggested.

In the bunker Reese sent Torres outside while he and Pierce talked with Snow. "It looks like your company was sent up here to die," Snow said. "But solely for the benefit of one individual in SOG headquarters, not for the good of the cause."

The S-3 handed Reese Clifford's letter outlining why A-410 had been sent to Dak Sang and what Marshall had hoped to gain from it.

"I'll be damned," Reese said softly as he looked up from the memo. "I knew that we'd pissed him off, or at least that I had. But I didn't think it would come down to this."

"There isn't much I can do about it after the fact," Snow said. "But you work for me now, and I don't allow things like this to happen to the troops under my command. I can assure you that this won't happen again."

Reese looked skeptical, but Snow continued. "This isn't for you to worry about, Captain. All I want you to do right now is to rebuild your camp and get your company back on its feet." The S-3 officer smiled thinly. "I'll take care of Marshall. You can count on that."

When Reese saw the smile on the Ice Man's face, he didn't want to know what the Hungarian had in mind. He knew it was better for him not to know.

"Yes, sir."

WHEN THE SLICK touched down in Kontoum, Laura was able to catch a ride on a C-130 Herky going in to Tan Son Nhut right away. After her plane landed at the air base and she stepped out, she was stunned by what she saw around her. Just a couple of hours ago she had been caught in the middle of a desperate battle, but Tan Son Nhut didn't look as though it were even in a war zone, much less a place that would ever fall victim to a battle. The contrast was staggering.

Outside the main gate she hailed a cab, gave the driver her address and sat back for the ride through town. Back in her Cholon apartment Laura didn't even stop to shower before she sat down at her typewriter. The story was written in her mind, and she had to get it down on paper before she lost any of it. She had to capture the sights and smells of the battle while they were still fresh in her mind.

She wrote of the American Special Forces men and their dedicated professionalism at the small hilltop camp, and of the Nungs who had fought and died fearlessly for the right to live free. She wrote of the terror of battle and of the countless small and large acts of bravery she had witnessed. She didn't leave anything out—her fear, the strange, terrible beauty of tracer fire, flares and explosions.

Then she vividly described the aftermath of the battle: the smell of blood and explosives, the blasted tank, the burned mess hall and the dead. And her mind kept going back to the dead, both the North Vietnamese and the Nung defenders. She had seen photos of casualties before, but she had never seen them in the flesh. Some of the men had looked like the immaculate dead in war movies, their eyes closed as though they were sleeping. But most of them looked more like slaughtered animals, their bodies torn to shreds and their eyes open and staring at what only the dead could see.

No photos could have ever prepared her for the smell of the dead. The overcooked meat smell of the burned tank crewmen, the sickeningly sweet odor of men who had bled to death and the butcher shop mixed with week-old latrine stench of the dead whose bodies had been ripped open by explosives.

When she typed 30 at the bottom of the last page of her manuscript, she knew she had finished the single best piece of writing she had ever done. Now she would shower and clean up before she edited the rough draft and typed a fresh copy to turn in to her editor that afternoon.

WHEN LAURA ARRIVED at her desk the next morning, she expected to find a blue-penciled copy of her story waiting in her in box for revision before it went out over the wires. But instead there was only an assignment to cover a story on reported drug use at MACV's in-country R and R center in Vung Tau. She frowned as she read the assignment. Maybe Edwards hadn't gotten around to reading her story yet.

"Laura?" Edwards called from the door of his office. "Can I see you for a minute?"

"What's up?" she asked.

"Your story," he said, waving the manuscript in his hand. "Have a seat."

She sat uneasily in the overstuffed chair across from his desk. "Is there something wrong with it?"

"No, not really," Edwards said. "It's a solid piece of work, really well written. But I've decided not to run it."

"What do you mean it won't be printed?" Laura was stunned. "Why not?"

"Well," he said, dropping the manuscript on top of the clutter on his desk, "there are two reasons, and I'll give you the most important one first."

Edwards leaned back in his chair with a smug smile, his eyes focused on her face for a change, instead of her breasts. "First off, Laura, I don't think you really understand the role of the press in this war, so I'm going to explain it to you. The sole job of people like you and me in Vietnam is to bring this war to an end as quickly as possible."

The reporter couldn't believe what she was hearing. "What in hell are you talking about?"

"It's real easy," the editor said, his voice assuming a regal tone. "The American people aren't behind this war at all, and it's certainly not in our best national interests. Therefore, as the voice of the American people, it's up to us, the press corps, to get this mess stopped as soon as we possibly can. One way or the other the war has to end and our troops have to be sent home. Your story, however, doesn't help us accomplish this goal."

"You're saying you want to end the war by manipulating the news?"

The editor shrugged. "We do it all the time, and you know it. We reporters—" he patted his chest proudly "—are the ones who decide what is and what isn't important in America, not our elected officials. National policy is what the press says it is, not anything the secretary of state says. Or the President, either, for that matter."

"But this is a good story," Laura argued. "It showed that part of the war here is going well, very well. It balances the doom-and-gloom stories we've been doing since Tet."

Edwards leaned across his desk. "Laura," he said seriously, "you're not listening to me. I know that you're relatively new to journalism and you're still full of that 'truth and honor' and 'all the news that's fit to print' crap they teach you in journalism school, but that's not the way it works out here in the real world."

"How does it work in the 'real world,' as you call it?"

"It's very simple," Edwards said. "The news is what we report, nothing more, nothing less. If we don't print it, it might as well have never happened. We're the ones who make history, not the participants. And, as you should know, bad news always sells better than good news."

"You're telling me that you won't run my story because it's good news?"

"There's more to it than that. I made a couple of phone calls and found out that even if I decide to run this, I might have a problem."

"How's that?"

"Well, it turns out that the Studies and Observations Group has friends in powerful places. I've been warned that if I print your story, this agency will be cut off from all of our official sources."

"But what about freedom of the press?"

"That's just more journalism school crap. That has very little application in the real world. This isn't some high-and-mighty crusade for truth and justice that we're involved with here. Journalism is a business, and we only yell about the First Amendment when it's to our advantage to do so." He paused. "And this time it isn't. We simply have too much to lose on this one. If we're cut off from our MACV sources, the competition will kill us."

"So you're telling me that you're caving in to blackmail?"

"I wouldn't exactly call it blackmail," he said smoothly. "I prefer to call it one hand washing the other. We simply can't operate here without MACV's cooperation. Look, I can give you some assignments with a little more meat to them if you'd like. Your story proved that you can write, but you have to write what we need, not things that'll get us into trouble."

Laura knew a bribe when she heard one. Edwards was openly bribing her with a real job if she would go along with what he saw as the way to keep from rocking the boat. "And what if I say I can't go along with this?"

Edwards leaned forward over the clutter of his desktop and smiled. "Then I'll just have to pull your press card and send you home."

Laura felt like telling Edwards to take her press card and shove it up his ass sideways. But the more rational side of her mind won out. This was no time for her to get herself fired, not when she had finally gotten in on the real war that was being fought in Vietnam. If she was declared persona non grata and sent home, she'd never get to write another story about the Special Forces. But if she kept her cool, she could play Edwards along until she could line up another employer, one who would let her write about the war as she saw it.

"I see your point," she said, trying to get just the right note of humility in her voice without sounding as if she were kissing his ass. "I guess I got a little carried away. This was the first time I'd even been close to something like that, and it had a real strong impact on me."

Edwards leaned back and smiled. He had known he would be able to bring her around to his way of thinking. He would have been really disappointed if he had been forced to ship her back to the States. He still harbored hopes of getting her softened up and taking her to bed someday.

"Good. Now we can get back to work on the important stuff. On this drug story in Vung Tau I want you to take your time. Pack your swimming suit, enjoy the beach, but get the goods on this for me."

"I will," she promised. "You can count on that."

24

July 6, Saigon

Colonel Stewart Marshall rode the elevator up to the third floor of the Brinks Hotel, his field-grade officer BOQ in downtown Saigon. It was well after curfew, but he was returning from an embassy party and had been driven in an official car. The party was the usual overblown embassy affair to welcome General Abrams to the Saigon military social scene, but he had been lucky to get an invitation.

Even though the new MACV commander was a tanker, Marshall had never really liked the abrasive, stocky Abrams. He had always found him to be entirely too blunt, boorishly outspoken and completely unpolished. And for the life of him, he couldn't understand how in hell Abrams had ever risen to the rank he had. An officer like him was better suited to commanding a brigade, not assigned to the top military command in the Army right now. Abrams didn't even have half the political or social connections Marshall did, and the colonel deeply resented that he was stuck in a do-nothing position while a man like Abrams ran MACV.

But now that he had secured a Legion of Merit medal for the Dak Sang action, his general's star was cinched. When he went back to the States, the Pentagon job he wanted would be his for the asking.

He put his key into the lock of room 306 and unlocked the door. He felt a bit of resistance when he opened the door and frowned. When he flicked the light switch on, however, his heart almost stopped.

His nightstand had been placed in the center of the room a few feet in front of the door. Sitting on the small table facing him was a claymore mine. A trip wire had been rigged from the mine to the inside doorknob, but for some reason the mine hadn't detonated. Heart pounding, he quickly stepped to the side, out of the line of fire, and fought to control his breathing.

He stood there for a long moment, uncertain about what he should do next. He was reaching for the phone to call the MP security detachment assigned to guard the hotel when he saw the red bomb burst patch with the grinning skull wearing the green beret lying on his pillow. The scroll under the bomb burst bore the letters *SOG*.

Marshall froze, the phone halfway to his ear, and stared. Slowly, carefully, he put the phone back down and backed away from the bed. It wasn't the VC who tried to assassinate him! It was someone from within his own organization!

He quickly crossed to the far side of the room and poured himself a stiff drink from the bottle on the desk. Sinking down into a chair, he sat and stared at the claymore. He had long since accepted the possibility of being killed by the VC. Any man who held his position ran that risk. But why this, an apparent assassination attempt from within his own ranks? What in hell had he done to warrant this? He knew he had enemies within SOG—that, too, was to be expected. But who hated him enough to want to kill him?

He knocked back half of his glass with one toss. They had missed him this time, but there was no telling when and where they would try again. If they could get into his quarters, it wouldn't matter if he had bodyguards and was extra careful where he went. There was, however, one thing he could do to make damn sure they didn't get another chance at him.

He had his Legion of Merit now, and maybe it was time he went back home. In the morning he would request an immediate transfer. If everything went well, he could be gone in three days. He stood up to refill his glass, then sat right back down.

The first light of dawn found Marshall sitting rigidly in the chair, an empty glass in his hands and his eyes still fixed on the claymore.

A BID FOR ULTIMATE POWER PITS NOMAD AGAINST A RUTHLESS TECHNOMESSIAH.

NOMAD

DAVID ALEXANDER

Code Name: Nomad—an elite operative trained to fight the ultimate technological war game. Waging high-stakes battles against technoterrorism, Nomad is a new breed of commando.

The year is 2030. The battle is over satellite-harnessed energy. The enemy is the supercomputer controlling the satellite network. This time, the game is real—and the prize is life on earth.

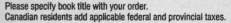

Take
4 explosive books
plus a
mystery bonus
FREE